P9-DZN-441

FOXCRAFT

✤ BOOK TWO ✤
THE ELDERS

❧ BOOK TWO ❧
THE ELDERS

CRAFT

BY
INBALI ISERLES

SCHOLASTIC INC.

If you purchased this book without a cover, you should be aware that this book is stolen property. It was reported as "unsold and destroyed" to the publisher, and neither the author nor the publisher has received any payment for this "stripped book."

Text and illustrations copyright © 2016 by Inbali Iserles
Map art by Jared Blando

This book was originally published in hardcover by Scholastic Press in 2016.

All rights reserved. Published by Scholastic Inc., *Publishers since 1920*. SCHOLASTIC and associated logos are trademarks and/or registered trademarks of Scholastic Inc.

The publisher does not have any control over and does not assume any responsibility for author or third-party websites or their content.

No part of this publication may be reproduced, stored in a retrieval system, or transmitted in any form or by any means, electronic, mechanical, photocopying, recording, or otherwise, without written permission of the publisher. For information regarding permission, write to Scholastic Inc., Attention: Permissions Department, 557 Broadway, New York, NY 10012.

This book is a work of fiction. Names, characters, places, and incidents are either the product of the author's imagination or are used fictitiously, and any resemblance to actual persons, living or dead, business establishments, events, or locales is entirely coincidental.

ISBN 978-0-545-69085-0

10 9 8 7 6 5 4   18 19 20 21

Printed in the U.S.A. 40
First printing 2017
Book design by Nina Goffi

FOR MY PARENTS,
DGANIT AND ARIEH
ISERLES—WISEST ELDERS IN
ALL THE LANDS.

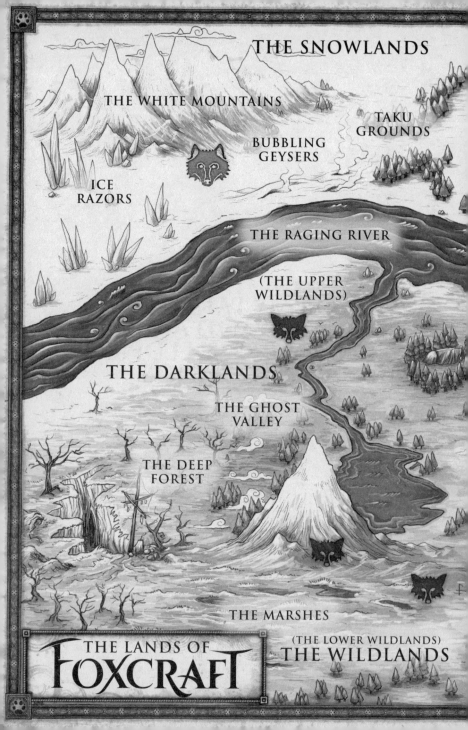

GROWL WOOD

TO THE SEA

THE WILDLANDS

THE ELDER ROCK

THE FREE LANDS

THE WILDWAY

THE BEAST DENS

THE GRAYLANDS
(THE GREAT SNARL)

ISLA'S DEN

THE DEATHWAY

Blando

1

I didn't stop when I heard the scream. At the edge of the forest, where the tall trees gave over to hunching bracken, I didn't delay and I didn't look back. The Wildlands buzzed with peculiar sounds: the hooting of birds, the braying of beasts. Tiny insects hummed in clouds and the grass hissed under the wind.

Great lands rolled out before me. In the distance I saw valleys, and hills that leaped sharply into the sky. A feeble sun hung overhead. Fields were exposed to watchful eyes, without the cover of trees. I would make for the mountain with its fringe of rocks, where I could cling to the shadows. From high over the Wildlands, I'd know where to go.

I picked up my pace.

But the scream tore through my thoughts. The hairs were stiff along my back, the breath sharp at my throat. A drop of rain fell on my nose and I quailed. A fox was begging for help.

I pressed through the bracken. *It has nothing to do with me,* I told myself firmly.

Since leaving the Great Snarl, I'd crept beneath trees in early bud, avoiding anyone I'd sensed on my path—even foxes. Once I had longed to be among my kind, hoping they'd help me find my family. Now I knew the truth: that my family was dead, except my brother, Pirie. He was lost to me in the vast green expanse of the Wildlands.

I would never see Fa, Ma, or Greatma again. Where my memories of them faded, a dark knot had taken root inside me.

I tried not to think of Siffrin, the handsome fox I'd met in the Snarl. He'd protected me from the Mage's killers— the Taken foxes with red-rimmed eyes. He had helped me catch prey, had led me to shelter.

I had come to think of Siffrin as a friend.

Trust no one but family, for a fox has no friends.

Greatma had been right about that. Siffrin had deceived me. He'd watched as the Mage's skulk killed my family. He'd let me believe they were still alive. He bore the scar, like a broken rose, the mark of the Taken at the top of his foreleg. A mark he had tried to conceal.

He had lied from the start.

My head peeked over the bracken. The first drop of rain was joined by others. They tapped against the leaves, bouncing and tumbling onto the ground. I paused, ears rotating. For a moment it was quiet, with only the shuffle of leaves in the wind, and the patter of rain from the darkening sky. Then the fox cried out again.

His voice broke into a series of yelps. "Help me! Somebody help me! I can't get out!" He started to whimper like a cub, though I could tell that he was full grown.

I stalked between the bracken, ears twisting this way and that. I couldn't work out where the voice was coming from. It seemed to be below me, almost as though it had burst from the belly of the earth. I tilted my snout. Up ahead was a tangle of hedge and ivy. Somewhere beneath it was the fizzle of water, perhaps a hidden stream. Was the fox down there? What was wrong with him?

I wove a path on tentative paws. Two ravens circled the sky, swooping in shimmering black feathers. One opened its beak with a *Kaah! Kaah!* As I neared the ivy, the rush of water grew louder. Nosing among the leaves, I caught my breath. The greenery fell away swiftly, the land plunging into a gorge. A stream gushed over the rocks below.

"Please help!" cried the fox. "I'm stuck!" I spotted him at the base of the gorge. He grunted, struggling to pull himself free. "I was chased by dogs and slipped down the bank. I didn't see it in time." He gave himself a shake and splashed back into the water. "I've caught my paw!"

He was wheezing and bucking but his hind leg was pinned between rocks. Ruddy water bubbled over his flanks. Overhead, the rain grew stronger. Rivulets coursed along the bank, swelling the tide below.

The fox was huffing and straining. "It's getting deeper. The rain . . ." He spat out a mouthful of water. My brush flicked with agitation as I traced the path of the stream. Dark rings ran along the bank of the gorge, high over the fox's head. Watermarks from previous showers. The stream would keep rising.

Trust no one but family . . .

The coarse fur flexed along my brush. I tensed to run. This fox had nothing to do with me. He wasn't my problem. I needed to keep myself safe, to focus on finding Pirie. I had to keep moving.

But my paws stayed planted to the ground.

I couldn't just leave him here to drown.

My eyes traced the top of the far bank, which was given over to leafy brush. "You said dogs were chasing you. Where did they go?" My muzzle wrinkled. I couldn't smell much but bark and soil. The sky trembled in the cool, clear rain.

"They saw me fall and they ran off barking. I guess they . . ." The gray-furred fox craned his head to look at me.

His ears flipped back. "You're only a cub." Disappointment edged his voice.

I crept along the ivy, looking for a foothold. "And?" I snapped. "I know more than you think." I'd learned some things since leaving my den in the Great Snarl. I had slimmered to avoid the watchful eyes of dogs, had karakked to confuse my prey. I had fed myself on mice and voles, caught with skill I never thought I'd possess. So what if it had been with Siffrin's help? I was managing without him now.

The clouds had drawn a veil over the day. Sunlight tumbled into night with scarcely a pause for twilight. The rain grew stronger, licking back my coat. I could see it rising along the bank of the gorge, rolling over the fox's shoulders. Curling about his throat.

The fox threw back his head and barked an alarm call, as though I wasn't there.

I slid a forepaw over the bank of the gorge. "Do you want my help or don't you?"

He peered at me through the gathering darkness. "Please . . . if there's anything you can do. I don't want to die down here. My family . . ."

A prickle touched my whiskers. I eased myself over the top of the bank, along the incline of the gorge. The earth was gooey, clinging to my paws in clumps and seeping between the pads. I slid down the bank. I moved slowly, bracing against clods of soil, blinking away the rain. The bank rose around me steeply. It wouldn't be easy to drag myself out but it was too late to worry about that now.

Water frisked and swirled below. All foxes could swim if it came to it—I knew that from Fa, who had loved a dip in the Wildlands when he was a cub. "Nothing better for cooling the pelt on a hot day." But I didn't relish the thought of springing into the stream. At least it was only the depth of the fox. His muzzle leaped up as he gasped for air, shaking away the water that splashed around him.

"I'm drowning!" he whined as I slid level with his neck, just above the water's edge.

"Stay where you are." It was futile advice—he wasn't able to go anywhere. Gritting my teeth, I pounced into the stream. The icy water nipped my belly. For an instant I sank under, panic clawing at me. Sight lapsed into bubbles, sound to a whoosh. A moment later I bobbed to the surface. The current pulled me away from the gray-furred fox, dragging me downstream. I beat my paws against it and hovered back, relieved to find that Fa was right—swimming came instinctively.

With a fresh surge of water, I bumped into the gray-furred fox. I scrambled to my paws to right myself. Swimming may have been instinctive, but it wasn't easy. The fox met my eye. The blacks at the center were slashes of terror.

"Please hurry," he whimpered. His muzzle craned upward as he gasped for breath.

I tried to duck down into the water but the current forced me back. With a deep breath, I sprang again, breaking the surface with my snout and kicking my legs so I sank beneath. Pressure snatched at my throat, but slimmering had taught me to hold my breath.

It was hard to see in the ruddy water. I reached out my senses as best I could as I pushed against the surge. Dimly I saw the contour of the fox's legs. One paw was pinned beneath a clutch of rocks. I made for it, seizing the largest rock between my jaws. It wouldn't budge and I floated back as the fox's free legs thrashed about me. The air pressed tightly at my chest. I tried again, stilling my mind.

Move, rock . . .

I willed it silently. A faint glow lit the gushing water. The fox stopped thrashing, making it easier for me to reach the rock. I felt the need for air now, clawing at my throat. With a final surge of energy I pushed toward the rock, clenching it again between my jaws. It shifted with a stubborn wobble and fell from my mouth. My head burst out of the water as I toppled backward against the stream. I launched myself onto the bank, gripping it with my claws as I gulped for breath.

The sky was gloomy with rain clouds. The stream rumbled on, growing higher beneath the downpour.

There was no sign of the gray-furred fox.

Had he sunk beneath the current? My ears pressed back. I remembered the two foxes in the cages at the snatchers', the ones left behind when I'd escaped.

I dragged myself up the bank of the gorge, my paws slipping against the sodden soil. It took the rest of my energy to hook my forelegs over the bank and heave myself up. I collapsed under a spiky hedge, my blood hot despite the bite of the stream and the steady patter of rain.

I pictured Pirie with his bright eyes and mottled coat. I wanted to see him as I remembered him, playing in the wildway near our den, chasing beetles in the long grass. I tried to recall his thrashing tail. But the image that came to me was different.

Pirie was close but concealed beneath a fog. As my thoughts melded with his, I could make out dim figures, menacing and unfamiliar. One took a step toward me and I caught the white glint of his fang.

Pirie's voice, very soft: I'm in trouble, Isla. There are shadows here, and trees with branches that catch like claws.

"I won't give up on you, Pirie! I'll find you, I promise!"

A gentle nudge stirred me from my trance. At once my eyes snapped open and my ears were alert. The rain still pattered against the hedge. Standing before it was the figure of a fox. The breath caught in my throat. It was hard to make him out with thick mud clinging to his fur.

I blinked in confusion. "Pirie?"

The voice that replied was not my brother's. "My name is Haiki. I think you just saved my life."

I frowned, momentarily confused.

"That hidden stream," he went on. "I slipped down and my paw got stuck. I don't know how you freed it, the rock was so heavy." He cocked his head, staring at me in awe. "What's your name, foxling?"

I blinked in surprise. He hadn't drowned after all. "I'm Isla."

The fox studied me for a long moment. Then he shook out his muddy fur, throwing a furtive look over his shoulder. His voice was low. "Those dogs . . . the ones that chased me. I don't think they went away after all."

My tail bristled. "Where are they?" I hissed.

A twig snapped a few paces away.

It wasn't a fox who replied from the darkness of the ferns.

"Right here," the dog snarled. "We've been waiting for you."

2

There were two scrawny dogs with narrow faces and jagged teeth. The one who'd spoken was larger, with dark brown fur. The other was black-and-tan with small, floppy ears. Both towered over Haiki and me. I could see ribs poking beneath their short pelts. In the Great Snarl dogs bullied foxes for sport, or at the command of their furless lords. These dogs looked shabbier than those in the Snarl. They were out after dark, with no sign of furless.

And there was hunger in their eyes.

Would a dog *eat* a fox? I shuddered, fear rising along my back. My gaze flicked over the shady bracken. There were plenty of places for a fox to hide, but we had to get away first. These long-legged dogs would easily outrun us.

Haiki edged closer to me, his face trained on the larger of the two. "You look like . . . like nice dogs," he said cheerily.

They stared at him in challenge. They looked nothing of the sort.

Haiki wasn't deterred. "We don't want to be any trouble," he went on. "We didn't mean to stray into your territory."

The larger dog took a step toward him. "But you *are* in our territory," he snarled. "Two foxes in a field. We're not fools. We know what you were up to. Chasing rabbits, that's what."

The second dog's eyes bored into us. "The rabbits here are *ours*."

I opened my mouth to protest. I'd seen rabbits in the distance but never tried to catch one. I didn't even know how.

"Our rabbits!" echoed the larger dog. He dropped his head with a growl, his hackles raised along his back. I swallowed, at a loss for words.

Haiki spoke quickly. "That was just practice, I was showing the cub what to do. Of course we'd never steal one of *your* rabbits!" His eyes jerked toward me, then back to the dogs. "It was just so *strange*, what the rabbits were doing. We couldn't help but watch."

The larger dog's muzzle crinkled. "Strange how?"

"Don't you know?" Haiki's eyes widened with surprise. "The rabbits . . . they all bounced over the field. I saw them, even the little ones. They were making for those, I think." He tipped his muzzle toward a distant jumble of hills.

The first dog gawped. "What do you mean, you *saw* them?"

My body was tense with fear. What was Haiki doing?

He gazed earnestly at the dogs, ignoring their threatening glares. "It looked like the whole warren. They were moving in a large group. Great big rabbits, lots of them, and little ones too. Just over there." Haiki threw a glance toward the open fields.

"The rabbits wouldn't leave just like that," rasped the black-and-tan. "What did you do to them?" He took a step closer, leveling up to the dark brown dog. I flinched, heart drumming. If I slimmered I might get away from them, but would it work when I was so close? How about Haiki? I could hardly leave him to the dogs, now that he was free from the gorge. Siffrin had slimmered over both of us on our first night together, hiding us from the Taken. My tail flicked behind me. I hated to admit it, but Siffrin's grasp of foxcraft was better than mine.

A lot better.

Haiki seemed to have a plan of his own. "We didn't do anything to the rabbits! Honestly, we just saw them. If you take a look now you'll see them too, a great many rabbits crossing in a group. No trees, no escape—they're just out there alone. Easy pickings." He ran his tongue over his muzzle with meaning.

The larger dog's head shot around toward the fields, but the view was concealed by ivy and bracken.

"Nonsense," snarled the black-and-tan. "Rabbits hate to get wet. Why would they choose to cross now?"

Haiki was quick to offer an answer. "Because it's dark, of course! They know that if they cross by day, you'd see them. Foxes would see them. Ravens would spot their young. It wouldn't be safe."

The larger dog was smacking his chops and craning his neck over the ivy. His tongue lolled out of the side of his mouth.

"Rubbish!" snapped the black-and-tan. "Why would they go at all?"

The larger dog frowned, his eyes growing hard. He turned back to Haiki. "Why would the rabbits leave?"

Haiki's eyes twinkled. "Why leave?" He paused a moment. My legs quivered nervously, but the gray-furred fox seemed to find his words. "Why leave, when two mighty dogs with fast legs and great teeth rule over this territory? If you were a rabbit, wouldn't *you* risk a night in the fields for the safety of the hills?"

It didn't make sense—rabbits lived beneath the ground, not high in the hills. Even I knew that, and I was from the Snarl. My ears pressed back. Haiki was flattering the dogs, and to my surprise it seemed to be working.

The dogs glanced at each other and took a few steps toward the fields.

"If you hurry, you'll catch up with them," said Haiki. "Imagine the feast. They say the young ones are especially tender . . ."

The larger dog was already prowling through the ivy, his thin tail wagging. The smaller dog started after him but paused, his head whipping round. "Stay here, foxes. If you're right about the rabbits, we may be kind enough to let you go. If you're wrong . . ." His lips peeled back to reveal his fangs.

"I know what I saw," Haiki insisted. "Trust me, you won't be disappointed."

I could hardly believe my eyes as the dogs disappeared through the bracken. I stood very still, Haiki watchful by my side. Then I dropped low on my haunches, preparing to flee.

"This way," urged Haiki. We started racing through the bracken, dodging hedges and roots, tracing a wide path outside the gorge toward the base of the mountain. We kept low, our tails brushing over the ground, beneath the line of foliage. The rain was easing up but I was grateful for its gentle tapping—it would help to conceal our scents.

Despite all I'd learned in the Snarl, I wasn't as fast as an adult fox. Gritting my teeth, I hurried to keep pace with Haiki. A short stretch ahead of me, the ferns petered out and the ground became rocky. Haiki paused at the edge of the bracken, waiting for me to catch up. I crept to his side, breathing heavily.

"The dogs are in that field," he murmured under his breath.

My ears swiveled forward and I traced the bleak horizon. Hills stooped beneath clouds, their outlines faint in the darkness. Before them I could just make out two figures, pacing and snarling in angry loops. A volley of barks burst from the dogs.

"Those foxes are dead!" the larger dog snarled.

But we were already far away.

In the Great Snarl, no place was beyond the touch of the brightglobes. The whole land hummed with their yellow light. Only here, in the Wildlands, did the night grow as black as a fox's ear-tips. In darkness we passed through a tunnel of ferns and reached the edge of the mountain. We stepped lightly over loose pebbles, hugging the land as we zigzagged uphill. The dogs would never find us now.

Haiki's pace slowed as we climbed the mountain. Deep furrows bored into its sides. I followed Haiki as he slunk along one and finally stopped to catch his breath. I sat a short distance away as he gnawed at clumps of mud from the gorge. Dust crumbled onto his tail, but he didn't seem to notice. He wasn't finicky like Siffrin.

After a moment he paused. "You saved my life, Isla. When I ran from the dogs, I tripped over some rocks and fell into the gorge. My paw . . . I couldn't free it. But somehow you did . . . such strength!" He cocked his head in gratitude.

"You got rid of the dogs, so I guess we're even." He'd succeeded not by fleeing, not with foxcraft, but through trickery. I had never seen anyone do that before.

In the distance, I heard a last angry yap.

"They said they'd seen us in the field, but that wasn't me." I glanced over my shoulder. "Is there someone else here?"

"No one I saw," said Haiki. "But dogs aren't the brightest!"

"Those rabbits weren't really crossing, were they?"

Haiki snorted. "In the rain? Of course not. Skittish creatures, rabbits. They can't stand water. But a dog is a greedy sort of beast—a dog will swallow anything."

The rain had drizzled to a stop. The clouds lifted, revealing a sky dappled with stars. Canista's Lights shone brighter than I'd ever seen them in the Snarl. I gazed overhead, mesmerized by the pulsing flares. I could make out shapes within patterns, faces and figures etched in white fire. Had the sky always looked this way, hidden behind the beam of bright-globes and the angry eyes of manglers? Or was it only in the Wildlands that the stars dared to sparkle?

"Beautiful, isn't it?" Haiki was watching me.

I wrapped my brush around my body. "I'm not used to such clear nights."

"What are you used to?"

I turned to look at him. Close up, I could see his gray fur was fuzzy at the edges, his limbs stocky and his face broad. I rose to my paws. "I should be going . . . But I'm glad you're all right." I stretched my back legs, preparing to leave.

"You should probably stay put awhile, in case the dogs come back. They'll be searching for us."

I paused, peering out over the edge of the rocks. The fields were so dark now that they looked like great hollow caverns. Somewhere in the distance, a creature hooted. It wasn't like any bird I'd heard in the Snarl. There was an accusation in its reedy voice, a warning to those down below.

I needed to climb the mountain to see what lay beyond— but even a fox's vision could not make sense of this vast, open blackness. I would have to wait until the sun rose over the horizon.

Haiki flopped down onto his belly with a yawn. "I can tell you're not from around here."

My tail-tip quivered. This fox may have gotten us away from the dogs, but I didn't know anything about him. Experience had taught me to be wary.

Haiki panted cheerfully. He stretched out a hind leg in order to groom it, but he tipped awkwardly, rolling onto his side and righting himself with a yip. "Me neither. I'm from the lowlands. I've been walking a long time."

"Why did you leave?" I shouldn't have asked. The less I knew about this clumsy fox, the easier it would be to leave him.

But Haiki seemed delighted at the question. He puffed out his chest self-importantly. "I'm on a quest! I'm crossing to the Upper Wildlands. I'm going to find the Elders!"

I looked away, catching the distant gleam of Canista's Lights.

"Have you heard of them?" asked Haiki in his quick, cheerful voice. He continued without waiting for a reply. "Where I come from, they say that the Elders are cleverest of *all* the foxes—they're the keepers of foxlore! They know practically everything." He dropped his voice, although there was no one around to hear us. "It's said they have powers. Strange magic . . ."

I dragged my eyes away from the lights. I thought of Siffrin, who had claimed to be a messenger for an Elder Fox. I remembered what he'd told me.

They are the guardians of foxlore, the wisdom and teachings of foxcraft. They are the seven wisest foxes of the Wildlands.

He'd said Jana, one of the Elders, was seeking Pirie. But Siffrin couldn't be trusted, and that meant that the Elders weren't to be trusted either. Still, I found myself asking, "Have you ever seen them?"

Haiki barked with amusement. "Seen them? Me, a simple fox from the lowlands? No one in my skulk has seen them. Some even doubt they exist, but I just know they do. We grew up hearing about them, me and my brothers and sister. We all loved the legends of the Black Fox—how he could turn himself invisible or shape-shift into other cubs of Canista."

My ears rotated. Siffrin had mentioned the Black Fox but I'd hardly been listening.

Haiki gave a wag of his brush. "That's the most powerful fox of all, the best at foxcraft. Have you heard about foxcraft?"

I murmured that I had.

He went on as though I hadn't. "It's how the Elders survived the cruelties of the furless. Each age has Elders and a very special Black Fox. This age needs one more than most, wouldn't you say?"

My ears flipped back. "What do you mean?"

Haiki seemed to contemplate me as though for the first time. "Where did you say you were from?" A wary edge had crept into his voice.

"From the south and across a bit, toward the rising sun."

"Not the Lower Wildlands?"

I chewed a claw in order to avoid his searching gaze. For some reason I didn't want to admit I was from the Snarl, though I couldn't imagine what difference it made. "The Graylands," I said shortly, using the term of the Wildlands foxes.

Haiki stared at me. "I've never met a Graylands fox before. What's it like there? Is it really as noisy and dark as you hear in the stories?" His eyes trailed over me. "Is that why you were so much better at moving the rock in the stream? Was it some type of . . . of Graylands foxcraft?"

"I don't know," I told him honestly. "I used the scraps of skill I've learned since leaving my den."

"You aren't with family?"

A shadow crossed my thoughts and I focused on my paw, gnawing away at a clump of dried mud. "I'm traveling alone."

Haiki leaped to his paws. "Me too!" He promptly sat, his tail jerking around his flank. "They've all gone." A whine touched his voice.

I looked up. "Gone?"

Haiki sighed. "All of them, the whole skulk. I was trying to catch this rabbit, you see. Not a normal rabbit! It had a fuzzy white tail, and white spots on its fur. I thought if I caught it I'd make Ma and Fa proud." He dropped his head onto his forepaws. "But the rabbit escaped down a hole . . . and when I got back, the skulk wasn't there."

A chill caught the back of my neck. It was like what had happened to my own family.

Haiki dropped his voice. "That's why I'm going to the Elders. If I want to find my family, I'm going to need help. I didn't know where else to go. The Elders are the cleverest foxes in all the Wildlands. They have to help me, don't they?"

I tipped my head in understanding. My voice was tight when I spoke. "Do you know where your family went?"

"I don't," he said quietly. "But I know they didn't leave by choice. And I know who took them. He must have used his wicked spells. His strange pale eyes, that shrub of a tail. He's the one who took my family."

A hiss escaped my throat. I didn't need to ask who Haiki meant.

Wicked spells . . . that shrub of a tail.

It was the fox who had ordered my parents' deaths. The one who had killed my Greatma. Stealer of wills, master of foxcraft. I still didn't know who he really was.

I only knew what Siffrin told me.

He built his den in the Deep Forest, hidden among ancient trees. They say he bends foxcraft to his command. The skulks from the Marshlands spoke of strange noises from the forest, odd smells and disappearances . . .

It could only be the Mage—the lord of the Taken.

3

The air about me felt sticky, trapped in a mizzling rain that carried no breeze. The cool sky didn't penetrate the web of vines between the branches. Peering overhead, I trained my eyes on the canopy, searching for shards of light. Was it day or night? No sunshine pierced the gloom beneath the trees, no hint of Canista's Lights. Only a faint yellow haze hung in the air, enough to capture shadows and cast them over the ground before my paws.

Beetles of terror crawled across my belly. What was this place?

Life as I knew it did not dwell here. No songbirds trilled in the branches—only the haunting caw of crows. I lowered my gaze. Nothing green dwelled on the forest floor. Not a single blade of grass. Instead strange mushrooms bobbed up from the earth like angry heads, shunting their way in the darkness. Invading the dank soil.

I sniffed one. Only a faint smell reached me, of something caustic and overripe. The fizz of acid coated my tongue.

"Watch out!" I yelped. "They're poisonous."

But when I turned to the fox by my side, his eyes were blank.

I woke with a growl in my throat.

"What's wrong?" A soft gray face was staring at me in alarm.

Dawn was rolling over the mountain. Its warming sun gave the rock a rosy flush and lit the tips of Haiki's fur. I could make out each whisker at his muzzle, each silvery hair along his flank. His pelt was longer than any I'd seen before. Despite his short, thick limbs his features were delicate: angular brown eyes, a narrow snout. My eyes settled on his foreleg.

What did I really know about this fox? Only what he'd told me . . .

I remembered the scar like a broken rose that I'd seen on all of the Taken—that I'd finally spotted on Siffrin.

On impulse, I sprang forward. Haiki recoiled but didn't strike as I shoved back the fur of his foreleg with my paw. Beneath the long gray hairs was a glimpse of pale skin.

I fell back, ashamed. "I'm sorry."

Haiki stared at me. "What were you . . . ? What was that about?"

I sighed. I would have to explain a few things. "I was just

making sure that you were . . ." I struggled to find the words. "Like me. That your will hadn't been stolen."

He cocked his head in confusion. "Stolen? How?"

I wasn't sure where to begin. "You told me about that fox who took your family."

He rose to his paws. "What about him?"

"Is he known as 'the Mage'?"

Haiki ran his tongue over his muzzle. "The Mage . . . Yes, that's him. I never saw him, but there were murmurings among lowlands foxes."

"I've heard things too. I've seen the Taken, and I heard that the Mage was responsible."

Haiki stared at me with his steady brown eyes. "The Taken?"

"The Mage's skulk, though it's bigger than any skulk I've heard of before. The Taken aren't like us. They don't think for themselves . . . They follow his commands like slaves."

There was something different about those foxes.

Something rotten beneath the skin.

"Their fur is bitter and smells of ash. Their eyes are lined in red and when you look inside you see nothing." I cleared my throat. "Whoever they used to be, they are hollow now. I hope your family was spared that fate."

Fear crossed Haiki's face. "I don't know what happened to them, only that they're gone. But I know it was the Mage. My skulk . . . They weren't the first. We heard rumors from

24

the Marshlands. Then the darkness came to us. My family disappeared, gone overnight." He shivered, despite the warming sun.

"Mine too," I whimpered.

Haiki's ears twisted forward. "The Mage took them?"

I gazed at my forepaws. "Those loyal to him tried. My family fought back . . . Only my brother escaped, but I don't know where he is. In the Wildlands somewhere. It's all so vast, even greater than the Snarl. I've been here for days and seen nothing but trees and fields."

"You mean . . . Your family's dead?"

"My brother's alive. I'm going to find him—I'm going to find Pirie."

"That's awful." He dipped his muzzle and gazed at me with sad eyes.

"I don't know who's loyal to the Mage, who's loyal to the Elders, or what it all means. So I'm wary." I said it as much for myself as for Haiki—I needed to remember to be careful.

"That thing you did to my leg . . ."

I ran a guilty tongue over my muzzle. "I'm sorry about that. I was checking you weren't one of the Taken. They bear a mark like a broken rose."

Haiki didn't reply right away. He stood and began pacing along the rock. When he spoke, it was over his shoulder. "Things are changing, Isla. I wish I didn't have to think about it . . . A fox can't live in this world and ignore it, not anymore. You and I are the same. We've both lost our families. Nothing matters more than family . . ." He turned suddenly, his eyes widening. "You should come with me to the Elders! They'll help us. You said it, the Wildlands are huge—bigger than any fox can imagine. You can't just go wandering without a plan. We *need* the Elders."

He gazed at me in appeal. I thought of the nights I had traveled alone, watchful and anxious in this unknown terrain. It felt like a lifetime since I'd walked by another fox's side, though it had only been days. That fox was Siffrin.

I tried to picture the Elders. Could they be trusted? Siffrin was Jana's messenger, and he'd lied to me.

A memory pricked my thoughts—Siffrin's anguished face as the snatchers pulled away in a mangler, dividing us forever.

Greatma's warning returned to me.

Trust no one but family . . .

I pressed my forepaw hard against the rock. "I have to do this alone."

The amber sun was climbing over the mountain. Soon it would highlight whatever lurked on the other side. A forest? A valley? The Wildlands were full of green expanses. My tail-tip tingled. Perhaps I lacked the Elders' wisdom, but I had a secret, a special power beyond the sight of others. I could reach out to Pirie through gerra-sharm. Our bond was so strong that our minds could interweave, collapsing distance through our thoughts.

The peak of the mountain disappeared into the clouds. It would take all day to climb but if I got there before sunset I'd be able to see in all directions. I would call to Pirie and he would guide me.

Haiki's tail was wagging like an eager cub's. "But we're both looking for our families."

My throat was dry. "Just my brother," I reminded him.

"Imagine it!" Haiki yipped. "The two of us across woodland and heath. You can tell me all about the Graylands, and I'll tell you stories from the lowlands. Soon there'll be rabbit cubs *everywhere*. Did you know that they're born without fur? The newborns are tiny, but so tender."

I frowned, my ears twisting this way and that. Had I heard a pawstep somewhere below? Rock was a difficult surface, like the graystone in the Snarl. Fallen leaves betrayed passing paws, but rock was silent. I craned my neck. It was hard to hear anything over Haiki's chatter.

"Though mice have been known to have cubs all year round, they're more active when it's warmer," he went on eagerly. "You can hardly prepare yourself for the taste of their cubs! My sister's an amazing hunter. She caught a litter once. She knew just where to look. They're quite hairless, you know, when they're born. Rabbits are too. Oh, I just said that! I wonder if that's why the furless don't have

27

pelts—they're cubs that never grew up?" He didn't wait for me to answer. "And then, another time . . ." He trailed off. He must have seen the look on my face. "Is something wrong? Ma says I talk too much."

"I think there may be—"

I didn't have time to finish. A furless rose over the edge of the rock, clutching a long brown stick. He was too far away to catch us, but there was something alarming about his frozen posture, and in the way he'd angled the stick toward Haiki.

A deafening explosion ripped through my ears. Haiki leaped from the furless as a burning hole cracked the rock above his head. I smelled fire and smoke, saw the furless rise and start chasing us, but no sounds reached me beneath the shriek of the stick.

I broke over the rock and pounded uphill. Blood pulsed at my throat as I scurried through crags and sprang over boulders. When I'd rounded a bend, I glanced back. Haiki was just behind me, his mouth twisted in a frantic yelp. I still heard the shriek of the stick, but beneath it I grasped his muffled words: "Run!" and "Hunter!"

Dizzily I lurched upward. Another look over my shoulder brought no sign of the furless, but I kept on going. My paws pounded over the sunlit rock, skidded on pebbles, and scrabbled to grip on to them.

Up I climbed, fear driving me on. As the rock crooked ahead of me, I saw flashes of a valley down below. Hedges clung to the side of the mountain. Their branches glanced my flank as I wove between them. Sunlight dazzled the rock, shining against my black forepaws. Haiki appeared at my side. A squirrel shot ahead of us and skittered up the rock face, staring down in alarm. I licked my lips but kept going.

At last I stopped on a smooth ridge of rock and Haiki flopped next to me. "Are you all right?" he panted. His words sounded muffled; the whine of the stick was still shooting through my ears. I shook my head violently.

"My ears," I mouthed.

Haiki blinked in understanding.

I looked up the incline of the mountain. It swept away steeply. Beyond it, the sun was high in the sky. Climbing was exhausting, and there was still so far to go. Turning, I surveyed the path behind us. There was no sign of the furless. I knew they couldn't run like foxes—it might take him half a day to reach us, and how would he track us? Greatma told me that they lacked a sense of smell. It was a wonder they survived without one.

I allowed my head to rest on my forepaws. Gradually, my breathing grew steady. Weariness edged through my aching muscles and I let my eyelids close. I found myself wondering about the Elders. Were they hostile, like the vixen I'd met on a wildway my first night alone in the Snarl? Were they thoughtful and wise, like Greatma? If they were really so mysterious, how had Siffrin grown close to them?

When I opened my eyes the sun had crept over the mountain. All around me, the rocks were burnished orange. Haiki was lying on his side fast asleep. As I yawned and stretched, he opened his eyes.

"How are your ears?"

The shriek had dulled to a hiss. "Better. How about you?"

His tail gave a wag. "I feel all right now. Glad we got away from that furless."

"I've never heard one make so much noise. He must have been furious."

Haiki shook his ears. "It wasn't him that made the noise, it was his stick. That thing can kill instantly. The furless have stumps for teeth and claws as soft as leaves. They use the stick to hunt."

I ran my eyes up the rocky path ahead. "I'm going to keep climbing. I'd like to see what lies beyond these rocks." *I have to get up there before the sun sets,* I thought. *I need to talk to Pirie.*

We took the rest of the mountain at a gentler pace, clambering carefully as the light deepened. Already the sun was bobbing lower on the horizon, throwing long shadows across the rocks.

By the time we approached the peak, I was ready for

another rest. The air up here was cooler, banked in cloud. A sputter of dampness touched my nose and I breathed deeply. We'd made it to the top of the mountain! I turned to look over the rock, creeping up a shallow incline.

Instead of a valley, I was greeted by a giant lake of glistening water. Far beyond it was a craggy hill, with outcrops of grass clinging to its borders. At the edge of the horizon, the sun was starting its slow descent. Its body hummed deep red, like a fox's pelt, and it trailed a violet brush. With a pang of sadness, I remembered how Siffrin's eyes lit up as he spoke of sunsets in the Wildlands.

My gaze trailed back to the lake. Even the strongest swimmer could never cross so much water, or survive the drop to the surface. A lip of rock overhung it, a cliff that loomed over the glittering water.

I looked at Haiki. "There's no way down." I couldn't conceal the disappointment in my voice. "We'll have to go back the way we came." My tail curved around my flank and my ears twisted sideways.

"But it's so far," Haiki sighed.

I craned my neck. Over his head, I'd caught movement. A shadow crept across the rock. A head loomed into view.

A furless with a long brown stick.

4

The furless was lowering his stick. I barked in alarm and Haiki whipped around, ducking behind a cluster of boulders. The furless grew still, his forelegs extended, his attention fixed on Haiki.

"Slimmer!" I yelped, forcing my heart to beat slowly. "Make yourself invisible." I was able to do it quickly now, gulping down my breath and quieting my mind.

What was seen is unseen; what was sensed becomes senseless. What was bone is bending; what was fur is air.

I felt myself drifting, fading from view. I pressed back against the rock, allowing my body to meld with its sharp gray lines.

Kaa-thump, kaa-thump.

But as my eyes rolled dreamily to Haiki, I saw him

scrambling against the stone wall. Was he crazy? Did he want to be killed?

"*Slimmer!*" Snapping at Haiki broke my own concentration and I struggled to stifle my breath.

"I don't know how!" he whimpered as the furless steadied the stick.

My gaze shot across the steep drop to the lake. I rushed to the lip of the rock. There was no way we could jump it, no chance we would survive the fall. I noticed a dark gap beneath the shaft. It might have been nothing, a dimple in the rock. I craned my neck. There was a small jutting boulder down there. Was it large enough to land on?

I crawled on my belly, tilting my head for a closer look. The gap slipped darkly into the rock wall.

I turned to Haiki. "This way! Quick!"

In an instant he was at my side. I heard the crack of the stick and a whistle as its fire roared over our heads. I slunk to the edge of the rockshaft. With a deep breath I launched myself off it, paws splayed to brace myself on the small jutting boulder. I landed with a thud, the boulder quivering under my forepaws. My back legs scrambled precariously over the lake. With a furious yowl I heaved myself up and looked straight into the gap I'd seen from above. It cut through the center of the rock. I scampered inside as another screech burst from the stick. Had Haiki made it?

I crouched in the gap, my ears shrilling. There was a small pool of rainwater by my paws, and I drank thirstily. From here, it was impossible to watch the shaft above. Had the furless caught Haiki with his deadly fire? I drew my brush around me and waited.

The stick shrieked, echoing through the rock. I craned my head over the edge of the gap to see Haiki spring onto the jutting boulder. Like me he landed awkwardly, his hind legs swinging over the drop. The boulder started tilting. With a scrabble of paws, Haiki dragged himself up and sprang toward the gap. As he thumped down by my side the boulder shuddered, breaking away from the rock with a growl. It lurched down to the lake. I heard a whoosh and a great distant splash as it sank under the water.

We panted at the edge of the gap, shaking away the cries of the stick. There was no sign of the furless, no way he could reach us under the rockshaft. Far below, the water shimmered on the lake, lit by the orange sun with its violet tail. The rippling vastness seemed to shrink the world around it. White birds bobbed on the surface, little more than specks from our vantage point. At least we were safe from the furless.

"He wasn't interested in me," I said at last.

Haiki let out a long breath. "He wanted my pelt. They always do."

I was relieved that I could hear him properly over the buzzing in my ears. I frowned, taking in Haiki's coat. In the Great Snarl, the furless did terrible things to us. I remembered the snatchers' mangler, which rounded up foxes and took them away to be killed. But I had never heard of hunters using sticks with fire. Did they steal pelts because they lacked fur of their own? I looked down at my paws and along my forelegs, where the black hairs turned ginger. Was there something about Haiki's coloring that made him more valuable to the furless?

He got up with a huff and edged toward the mouth of the gap. Lapping at the puddle of water, he looked out over the lake. He took in the lip of rock above, then he turned to me. "We can't go back where we came from. We can't go forward."

I stared into the darkness of the gap, which seemed to reach into the heart of the rock. But how far did it go? What if it ended at a stone wall? We'd be stuck here, waiting to starve. I shuddered and rose to my paws, treading into the darkness. Haiki followed.

We had no choice. There was nowhere else to go.

The passage was narrow. It wasn't long before the light faded. The walls blackened and disappeared. I padded warily, listening for unusual sounds, hearing Haiki's pawsteps just behind me. He seemed to make an effort to stay close, as though he was afraid of the dark.

"I can't believe you know foxcraft," said Haiki. His voice echoed along the passage. "Back where I'm from, only a few foxes do, and they're not the young ones. Did you learn to slimmer in the Graylands?"

"Yes." It was true, although it wasn't the whole truth— I'd learned it from Siffrin, a Wildlands fox. But no one had taught Pirie how to slimmer; he'd grasped it instinctively. "I can karak too," I added. That made me feel better. I'd learned how to mimic the calls of other creatures all by myself.

"Amazing," sighed Haiki. "I don't know any foxcraft . . . Ma always said, 'If you're in a trap and you fear a bite, use your cleverness, not your might!'" He panted with amusement. "A fox is smarter than other sons and daughters of Canista, but he isn't as strong. There's no point getting into fights."

I remembered how Haiki had tricked the dogs. But without being able to slimmer, he'd been helpless in the face of the furless. Beneath Haiki's cheerful chatter I sensed frailty.

My ears pricked up and my whiskers edged forward. I looked back over my shoulder. The last glimpse of light from behind us cast a glow around Haiki. Only his eyes shone against his long fur. For a beat, I lost my footing. The silvery gleam beneath his thick lashes made him look sharper, more cunning than he'd seemed.

"It's a cave." My voice echoed along the rocks and my ears flicked back.

"But where does it go?" asked Haiki. "You won't leave me here, will you, Isla?" His voice crackled with anxiety. I felt a curious impulse to protect him. I drew in my breath, focusing on the unfurling darkness. I couldn't leave the gray-furred fox, not now at least. Not until we reached open land.

The passage cut deep into the rock. We walked a long time. I felt the ground rise beneath my paws, then stagger downhill. What if it simply fell away?

"It's pretty tight in here," said Haiki. "I don't like being in closed spaces. Do you?"

"Not much," I said shortly. I wanted to focus on the messages from my paws and whiskers. My brush swished, flicking against each wall. Was the air growing thin? The ground was lurching at an angle. I thought I heard the distant gush of a stream. I smacked my lips thirstily and paused, ears straining.

Haiki stumbled into me. "What happened?" he yelped.

"It's all right," I soothed. "I thought I heard water."

We both stood still in the darkness. Silence seemed to stretch in all directions. Perhaps I'd been wrong.

I started padding down the incline and sensed Haiki following close behind. A couple of times, my brush swept against him as I felt for the distance of the walls. They were growing narrower. The air smelled damp. Despite breathing hard, I could scarcely fill my chest. Fear crept along the back of my neck as each step took me deeper into the unknown. My head felt light. My heart quickened against my ribs. I had a sudden impulse to turn and bolt, to throw my paws against the wall and claw my way to freedom.

Greatma's voice drifted through my thoughts.

Fear is your friend, but it must never be your master. It will leash you just as surely as the furless do their dogs, and drag you to an even darker fate.

The hairs spiked along my brush. I couldn't remember Greatma ever giving me such a warning. It was almost as though I could actually hear her. Like I could *feel* her. My whiskers bristled and my mouth parted in wonder. "Where are you?"

It was Haiki's voice that responded. "Right behind you."

"I thought . . ." I blinked hard into the darkness. The thin air was making my thoughts fuzzy. I forced myself to breathe slowly. My ears pricked up. "Can you hear that?" A burble, a babble, like the patter of rain.

"Water!" gasped Haiki.

The ground leveled out beneath my paws. The sound of running water grew stronger. It wasn't rain—it was the voice of a stream. In my excitement, I picked up the pace and smacked my snout into a wall of rock. Fear scurried over my back once more: the passage was blocked; we were trapped!

Greatma's voice:

38

Don't let it become your master . . .

"What's wrong?" hissed Haiki.

I lapped at my sore nose, listening for the flow of water. It wasn't far away, just beyond the wall of rock. I reached out a forepaw, hooking it around the hard stone. There was a narrow gap between the rocks. I slid my head through, blinking against prickles of light. A slender stream tumbled over a gap in the rocks. The air was cool and fresh.

My tail started wagging.

I drew back, turning to Haiki. "Just up ahead, the rock bends. I think there's a way out!"

"There is?" Haiki bounded forward, bumping me against the wall in his excitement. He shoved his head around the stone. "Oh, well done, Isla!" He fell back, allowing me to slide through the gap and out into the open. I took in great gulps of clean air. Even the murky light of dusk ached against my eyes.

I heard a grunt behind me. Haiki was struggling to slip between the narrow walls. "Almost there," he muttered. He squeezed his way out with a triumphant squeal.

Together we slipped through the shallow stream, the icy water cleansing our coats. We had arrived at an outcrop of rocks at the edge of the lake. A narrow path cut between them, earthy and dank.

We must have been inside the rock a long time. Twilight coated the still water. I gave myself a shake. My eyes were fixed on the lake but I wasn't really seeing it—I was remembering my patch, back in the Great Snarl. Thinking of the meeting of day with night, when we'd shuffle from the den to explore the wildway.

I remembered an evening long past, when Pirie was hunting for beetles. He was snaking through the grass, his tail bobbing up and down, disappearing from view.

"Got one!" he yelped. I ran to his side, smacking my lips. Pirie was trying to grasp a huge beetle that was doing its best to creep up the trunk. It pulled itself free from my brother's grip, but I batted it back with my forepaws. It tumbled to the grass, rolling back on its hard shell. We watched as it kicked pathetically, unable to right itself.

I made a move toward the beetle. "I'm taking it to Ma and Fa."

"I found it!" Pirie went to block my path. "I'm the one who'll take it."

Ma's voice rose over the grass. "Isla! Pirie! It's raining. Come back to the den."

I hadn't even noticed the rain. Now I looked up to see the sky was murky. Drops slid onto my nose. I scowled at the streaky clouds. They always meant we had to go inside. Why couldn't the rain just leave us alone?

The beetle was swaying on its shell. With an effort, it rocked onto its legs and started tumbling through the grass. I pounced but Pirie was still in my way. I smacked into his flank and tried to reach around him, but the beetle had scut-tled away.

"You let it go!" I snapped angrily.

Pirie's ears flicked back. "You were closer."

"Isla! Pirie!"

My ears flattened as I turned toward the den. Now we had nothing to show Ma and Fa. The rain was growing stronger, splashing onto the grass and sliding down the bark of the tree, *gurgle-splash*.

Gurgle-splash.

A fish broke the surface of the lake, washing away my memory. For an instant, I saw its lidless eye before it shot into the murky depths. Echoes of movement in endless ripples.

I sighed, my tail curling around my flank. The memory of my squabble with Pirie saddened me. I should have let him take the beetle. He was right: he had found it.

"I'm sorry," I murmured. My whiskers flexed as I reached out with my senses, hoping to feel his presence. "Are you there?"

"Did you say something?" It was Haiki, not far behind me. "It's quiet here, isn't it? Reminds me of this time when I was a cub—"

"It was nothing." I shuffled closer to the bank of the lake. I wasn't about to tell Haiki that I was trying to reach my brother through gerra-sharm—it was none of his business. I drew in my breath. In my mind's eye, I pictured Pirie's mottled coat, golden-brown with splashes of flame. The creamy fur inside his ears, the black that touched their outside tips.

The water of the lake grew still.

Isla? Something's happening to me . . . I don't feel the same.

I caught my breath. His voice in my head was soft as a whisper. The world around me darkened. The outlines of trees wove over my vision.

There were branches and shadows. A bitter dust filled the air. It crept into my nose and sank down my throat.

I drew in a long breath and the image faded. But a sense of dread lingered. "Pirie, where are you?"

I don't know anymore . . . I'm starting to forget.

His voice was blurred by a curious hissing, like the wind in dry leaves. My head felt light, a muddle of colors and twisting thoughts. Pirie running free in the wildway; Pirie alone in a dark land.

"What are you forgetting?" I murmured.

Everything.

My ears quivered. I didn't understand.

I think it's time that you forgot too. Let me go, and live your life. Turn back. Don't look. It isn't safe.

"I'll never forget you!" I yelped.

"Isla? What are you saying?"

I blinked hard. The colors dissolved and my thoughts grew steady. The lake lapped lazily against the rock bank. Haiki was standing by my side, a curious expression on his face. He gave me a gentle nudge with his nose. "You were talking to yourself."

I ran my tongue over my muzzle. What had he heard?

I rolled onto my paws. "This way."

Haiki trotted behind me.

The path strayed away from the water and we followed in silence. My belly rumbled. I promised myself I would hunt down a mouse when we reached a meadow.

The path cut between the rocks till they opened onto a clearing, a valley at the base of the mountain. I paused to sniff the ground. It was mulchy under my paws, falling into scrubland. A low wind whipped between the rocks, blowing twigs and dried leaves toward me.

Nothing green grew in the valley.

The russet grass was patchy, as if scorched by a hostile sun, though the ground was damp and the air was cool. The odd withered vine bucked over the soil, ropy and raw like a rat's tail.

The last murmurs of dusk hung over the horizon. A faint scent prickled my nose, of rotting bark and withered leaf. My belly growled with disappointment. I couldn't imagine a mouse living here—what would it have to eat?

Haiki was gazing over my shoulder. "I don't like the look of this place."

I glanced across the valley. "Let's cross quickly. I think I see trees over there. It might be a forest." I had passed through a wood on the borders of the Snarl. I knew that small creatures dwelled under the trees. Squirrels made their nests there. Birds trilled in the branches. I smacked my lips. Down in the soil, the worms were plump and bugs provided an easy snack.

We started over the valley. Dead shoots sagged beneath my paws. The smell of decay grew stronger, stinging my nose. We slunk past small mounds of rotting matter. As I passed one I made out a slab of bark and some scrunched-up leaves. A tiny skeleton was half-concealed by soil—a mouse or a vole. Oozing over the slender bones was a slug. I paused to sniff the mound, whiskers flexing. The slug was the first living thing I had seen in the valley. It smelled faintly acidic.

I moved away quickly toward the distant trees.

Between bowing grass stems, I spotted a small yellow bulb. I'd seen one before, but I couldn't remember where. As I drew closer I noticed others: an invasion of stooped yellow mushrooms with purple speckles, shunting their way through the soggy earth. I padded toward one, nostrils pulsing.

"Keep away from them!" spat Haiki. I shrank back in surprise—I hadn't heard him use that tone before.

"Why?"

Haiki had frozen in his tracks. "You mustn't eat them. They'll make you sick." He raised his muzzle, blinking toward the trees, where the last streak of sunlight sank from view. The mushrooms were pale and fleshy against the dark floor of the valley. "I don't think we should be here."

I saw the look in his eyes, caught a whiff of his scent. Fear was rising from his coat.

"Once we get to the trees—"

"We should leave now, find another way." Haiki's fur rose along his back. His tail crept to his flank.

My whiskers quivered. He was scaring me. "What's wrong?"

Haiki started shrinking backward, low to the ground. "Don't you hear it?"

"Hear what?" I strained my ears. The air was quiet except for the breeze that shrilled through the rocks at the base of the hill.

"Exactly," he hissed. "The silence."

I tipped my head. Haiki was right—this was the Wildlands. Where was the buzz of insects? Where was the twitter of birds?

My eyes scanned the valley, searching for a sprig of greenery, a spark of life. Even the distant trees looked hunched and sickly. There was no sign of buds in their branches.

As my eyes trailed over their trunks, a figure appeared

from the gloom. One more stepped out alongside him, then another.

They prowled in formation. Their pointed ears craned forward, their bushy tails straight behind them. It took me a moment to realize they were foxes. There was something stiff about their postures, something mindless in the way they stalked, lowering their heads and arching their backs.

Haiki must have sensed it too. "Who are they?" he whispered. There was a tremble in his voice.

I struggled to make out the marks on their forelegs or the smell that clung to their coats like ash. From this distance I couldn't see their eyes. But a dark instinct told me they'd be red-rimmed and blank.

"The Taken," I gasped as they started toward us across the rotting valley.

5

A groan rose from the twisted trees. I stumbled, my tail snagging on thorns. Shapes grew distorted in the half-light. Vines shuddered on the wind, like rats' tails slinking around my legs. The mushrooms swiveled their bulbous heads in my direction. Were the trees creeping closer, extending their jagged branches, curling and arching them like claws?

The stench of decay grew stronger. An old fox stood among the trees, watching the Taken march over the valley. Even from a distance, I could see the acid blue of his eyes.

My tail fell limp.

The groan of the valley deepened. Specks of yellow dust seeped between the twisted trunks, drifting toward me on the wind. Breath rattled at my ears and my mind grew blurry. It was almost as though the old fox was inside me, clawing at my thoughts.

"Isla! Are you all right?" Haiki's voice was urgent.

I blinked hard. When I looked again, the old fox had vanished. The groan dulled enough for me to hear the approach of the Taken as dry leaves crunched under their paws.

"Where did he go?" I gasped.

"Who?" Haiki frowned. "What's wrong with you?" He pawed me, nipping my flank.

I shook my head and blinked again. They were creeping closer, a dozen foxes or more, their sloping steps unhurried. I tried to lift my foreleg. It felt heavy, as if tugged to the earth by vines.

"This way," Haiki insisted, leading me toward the edge of the mountain. Obediently I followed, trying to shake away the wooziness that had seized my thoughts. "Look at me," said Haiki. "Follow my brush." I fixed my attention on the gray-furred fox as he picked up speed.

I was faintly aware of the Taken foxes. Aware that they too were moving faster, hurrying to meet us in the gray pall of dusk. My eyes shot to the sky. Dark clouds had sprung from nowhere to conceal Canista's Lights.

I struggled after Haiki. His fur blended with the grimy light. Only the white tip of his tail stood out, twitching like a separate beast. I glanced toward the stalking skulk. A ginger fox was drawing near. As his red-rimmed eyes met mine, I caught the shiver of Pirie's voice.

Turn back. Don't look. It isn't safe.

The fox's eyes seemed to glow, and I felt my paws slowing on the ground.

"Isla, keep moving!" Haiki was staring at me in astonishment. "It's a trick! A wicked foxcraft."

I broke from the power of the fox's stare. I saw the flash of Haiki's tail and ran at it with all my might. He started forward again and I sprang after him, my heartbeat pounding in my ears, drowning out the groan from the trees.

Haiki rounded the bend at the base of the mountain and I followed. Up ahead there were sprigs of grass and shoots that bore new life. The rotting earth lost its grip on me, its rumbling groan fading from my thoughts. Dusk had fallen to night, and with it the creeping haze of the valley. Canista's Lights broke through the clouds and I felt myself grow stronger. In an instant I smelled grass and fern, saw flowers bursting from the soil. A wave of elation rushed through me.

I focused on Haiki's bobbing white tail-tip and thought of the Lights overhead. I felt soft grass beneath my paws and heard the song of a night bird. The rotting valley fell behind us, along with its acrid odors and haunting sounds. We'd outrun the Taken. We were almost free.

Haiki slammed to a halt. He whipped around to face me, his eyes full of dread. "They've cut us off," he panted.

I blinked through the darkness. Two foxes bounded toward us, blocking the path ahead. Beyond them I caught the swell of a green meadow. A thicket of dense shrubs swayed on the breeze, easily deep enough for us to hide inside—and tantalizingly out of reach. The foxes slowed as they approached, their red-rimmed eyes catching the light of the moon. The first was a long-eared, bony vixen, the second a male with short fur. Dark red grooves were etched on their forepaws.

The mark of the broken rose.

There was a shuffle of steps close behind us—the rest of the skulk as they circled the hill.

Haiki stumbled into me. "Oh no," he whined. "We're surrounded!"

The two foxes ahead of us came to a halt. The wiry male looked in worse shape than the vixen. Sallow froth bubbled at his jaws and gunk clumped on his eyelashes. His whiskers were strangely still, his red-rimmed eyes unblinking.

I thought of Tarr in the snatcher's den. Were other eyes peering through this fox's gaze, telling him what to do?

Haiki backed into my flank, his haunches quivering.

I heard an anxious whine behind me. The foxes were turning, hackles raised, peering toward the dark valley. Something was distracting them. I trained my ears. At first there was only the song of the lonely bird. Then a burst of yelps caught the air. The yelps broke into a shrill howl. My ears flicked back. It wasn't the cry of a fox. It wasn't like anything I'd heard before.

Toward the rear of the skulk, someone barked. "The Master wants the trespasser, dead or alive!"

The others gekkered, a luminous tinge in their eyes. Their high-pitched clicks sent the bird flapping away in fright.

"Catch the beast that is not what he seems!" screeched a fox in the middle of the huddle. They began to retreat from me and Haiki, running in the direction of the yelps. Their paws slipped as they rounded the hill and dissolved into shadow.

I turned to Haiki, trembling with relief. "They've gone! The Taken have gone!"

His gaze was fixed on the disappearing skulk, his muzzle pulsing. He didn't seem relieved. He looked wary.

"You are mistaken." The bony vixen had spoken. She stood a few paces ahead of us. Her paws were planted on the ground, her hackles raised. The male fox leveled up beside her, baring foam-caked jaws.

They hadn't left with the others.

They took a step toward us and Haiki arched his back, trying his best to look threatening. It did nothing to deter them.

Even two of them could overpower us. I was still a cub and Haiki gave no sign of being a fighter. If only I could perform wa'akkir, the shape-shifting foxcraft. If only Siffrin had taught me that.

I felt a flare of rage at the red-furred fox and used it to focus my mind. Ears forward, I drew in my breath. I spat it out in a series of angry caws. The sound of crows filled the air, whirring around the two red-eyed foxes. They froze in their tracks with uncertain glances. Haiki whined in surprise, his ears flattened. He started to spin in a tight circle, panicked by my karakking. I wanted to tell him it was only me but I didn't know how without betraying the secret.

I fixed on the Taken. With another breath I showered dog barks upon them, drawing great woofs and snarls from my throat. Haiki started to back toward the rotting valley. Quickly I thrust myself forward, away from Haiki, into the path of the red-eyed foxes. Controlling my breath, yet spitting out barks, I started to slimmer.

All color drained from my body and the contours of my limbs grew vague. I crept around the bewildered foxes, who could no longer see me and whimpered in fear. I let the sounds swirl around them, capturing them in a net of confusion.

Slimmering and karakking at the same time was harder than I'd anticipated. I hadn't eaten, and the escape from the gorge had drained my maa. I could feel the power of my slimmer failing. In a few beats my body would regain its shape and color. Even now, the black fur of my forepaw flickered back into view.

Despite their fearful faces, the foxes weren't backing away. They whimpered but held their ground.

With a last great effort I spat out the howl of a savage dog preparing for battle. It was too much for the male fox, who fled from the sound. He bolted past Haiki, in the direction of the valley. The vixen dared not stay alone amid the clamor. With a shriek she dashed after him, back toward the mushrooms.

I released the slimmer, gasping for breath. My head drooped and I squeezed my eyes shut, feeling giddy.

"It was you!" gasped Haiki, his voice drifting down to me. "Those foxes came, so many of them, and *you* scared them away! You know foxcraft! I mean, you *really* know it. A cub from the Graylands, who'd have thought . . . ?"

I'd only scared two of the Taken. The rest had run on hearing those eerie cries. But I let Haiki burble on, too feeble to correct him, as I dragged myself toward a patch of hazel at the edge of the meadow.

"You really are different, aren't you, Isla?" he asked, wide-eyed and playful. He didn't wait for a reply. "My brothers and sister are clever. They're good at hunting, but they're older, of course, and none of them could do what you did!" He bounced at my side.

Secretly, I was touched by his praise. Foxcraft *was* hard. Slimmering and karakking at the same time had taken all my concentration. Siffrin had done nothing but insult me. Haiki was altogether easier to travel with, even if he did talk too much.

I nosed among the hazel, drinking in its soft, fresh scent. I could sense the life in its thick stalks and small buds, so different from the rotting brown expanse of the valley. Slipping into the bushes, I padded a circle and lowered myself onto the ground. My body was weary but my mind felt gentle relief.

Haiki curled up alongside me and I didn't protest. It felt good to be close to a fox again.

"We'll find them," he murmured.

I blinked at him.

He gave me a nudge. "My skulk, your brother. We'll help each other . . . We'll find them somehow."

A quiver of hope trembled at my whiskers.

Canista's Lights had melted behind banks of cloud. I breathed deeply and closed my eyes. The darkness of the night was like the velvet of my thoughts.

I woke to see brown eyes fixed on me, intense beneath the light of the moon. Haiki brightened when he saw me watching him. "You're awake! You were sleeping so heavily, I was worried. Is it because of the foxcraft? Are you all right?" His fluffy tail thumped the soil beneath the hazel bush.

My head felt heavy. "It takes a lot of maa," I murmured. I could have easily slept all night.

"I'm *so* hungry, aren't you?" Haiki yawned noisily. "All that running, and those horrible foxes . . ." He shuddered. "But I've been keeping a lookout and they didn't come back." His gaze dropped to his belly and his soft gray ears pointed sideways. "I haven't eaten all day."

My own belly groaned. Now that I was awake, I was famished. It was still dark beyond the branches of the hazel bush. "I guess we have to hunt."

"Yes, hunting . . ." Haiki shook his head sadly. "I'm not good at that, though I muddle by."

I sighed, flexing my forepaws. Why didn't that surprise me?

He leaped to his paws like a cheerful cub. "Shall we try to find rabbits?"

"In the middle of the night?"

"True, that's pretty impossible."

My tail twitched impatiently. Hunger wasn't improving my mood. I'd never even seen a rabbit up close. They were fiendishly fast.

"We'll find something," I muttered halfheartedly, wondering why I was still with the gray-furred fox. I had promised myself I would travel alone. I stretched and rolled onto my paws. My forelegs quivered and my limbs felt heavy. Was I strong enough to hunt?

Haiki was watching me with concern. "You don't look too good. What happened to you in that valley? I had a bad feeling, then those foxes appeared from nowhere." His tail stopped wagging and sprang to his flank. "And you seemed . . ."

"I'll be fine." I brushed away his words with a flick of my tail. But the truth was something *had* happened to me. I'd heard sounds, seen things, was ensnared in a trance. Who was the fox with the acid eyes who'd watched from the trees? I recalled the rattling in my ears, as though his breath was raking my mind.

Gerra-sharm was a rare foxcraft, one of the forgotten arts—Siffrin had taught me that much at least. My bond with Pirie allowed me to reach him with my thoughts. Through gerra-sharm we were one, our minds melded together. The sensation in the woods had felt similar . . . but awful. Like my own gerra was being sapped. I couldn't think straight, could hardly raise my paws.

I shook my head fiercely, freeing myself of the memory, and pressed between some hazel stalks.

Haiki started after me and we trod through the long grass together. As we climbed over exposed roots, I thought I heard the scratch of tiny claws on earth. I trained my ears, my whiskers edging forward. It was probably a mouse.

"Rabbits are delicious," Haiki began. "I could eat a whole one right now, I really could! My sister caught this great big rabbit. We couldn't believe it, so succulent."

There was a frantic scrabble of little paws—the creature had heard us. I shot an angry look at Haiki.

"I'm sorry, was I talking too much?" His brush drooped behind him.

We carried on in silence, crossing the meadow and winding between trees. In time we approached a curving hill, then a valley of shrubs and thorns. A narrow stream ran through the valley.

I wavered uncertainly. A faint scent of foxes hung in the air.

Haiki kept going. "Oh, look, at least we can have a drink."

I licked my lips and followed. We stopped to lap the water. It eased my parched throat but my legs ached worse than ever, and my head was beginning to thump.

Haiki watched me. "You're too tired to hunt."

It was true, but what choice did I have? I didn't trust him to find food for us. For a moment I wished Siffrin was here. The red-furred fox was good at hunting, an expert in stalking without being seen. My ears rolled back. I reminded myself he was also a liar who bore the mark of the broken rose.

Haiki trod toward me and gave me a gentle nudge with his muzzle. "You need to rest." His eyes lit up. "Wait a moment!" He started treading over the grass, his snout close to the ground. He took a couple of deep sniffs and walked on a few paces, sniffed again, and rounded back. I watched, head cocked, as he stopped above a patch of soil where no grass grew. It looked freshly disturbed.

I peered into the surrounding grassland. The stream hissed over the meadow and bats circled in the darkness. Had I heard something else? My ears twisted. Again I sensed foxes. Had we strayed into someone's patch?

Haiki started digging with an eager jerk of his tail. Soil sprayed behind him. Ears pinned back; forepaws a blur of gray fur.

He buried his muzzle in the dirt and yanked it out with a triumphant yip. "You won't believe what I've found!"

A rich, sweet smell was rising from the soil. Saliva filled my mouth and my belly rumbled as Haiki's head disappeared once more. His back legs tensed, his rump quivered, and he backed up with a shake. Tail lashing, he dropped a mound before me.

I could hardly believe my eyes. Beneath the crumbling soil I saw a long, floppy ear, a furry body, and a creamy tail. *A rabbit!*

Its head hung heavily, its neck already broken.

"You first. You're starving." Haiki dropped the rabbit in front of me. "Plenty for both of us."

I quivered with anticipation, too ravenous to question this gift from the earth. I grasped the pelt in my teeth and sheared off a chunk of meat. It was still warm. Haiki sank his jaws into a hind leg. We growled and tore, ripping off great strips of rabbit and swallowing them whole. It didn't take long to gobble most of it down, leaving a small mound of gristle and bone.

With a sigh of contentment, I looked up at Haiki. The rabbit's blood clung to his muzzle, reddening his whiskers. Haiki licked his chops. A full belly made me generous. *I've been too hard on him.* Maybe he couldn't hunt, but he had found a dead rabbit! And he'd looked out for me in the rotting valley. I remembered how he'd beckoned me away from the Taken. He might have abandoned me and saved his own pelt.

The slightest stirring of the soil and my ears pricked. Over the hiss of the stream came another sound. The careful tread of a fox's paw. My head shot up to meet furious eyes.

Haiki whined and backed toward me. The fox stood over us, a powerful male with a ruddy coat. Black fur circled his eyes, making them look impossibly large. They trailed over the remains of the rabbit.

"Thieves," he spat. His face contorted with hatred. "Slaves of the Tailless Seer. You poison our valleys. You terrorize our dens. And now you dare to steal our food! Long have I waited to catch you at your mischief. Long have I yearned to rip out your throats." His tail shot out behind him. He raised his muzzle and barked an alarm call. I felt a rumbling beneath my paws, a shunting of earth and roots. All of a sudden foxes appeared, bursting out of hidden tunnels.

The ruddy-furred male addressed them. "These thieves are pleached! Don't let them escape! I heard them crossing the Ghost Valley. And now they've arrived at our patch. What should we do with them?"

"Kill them, Flint!" the foxes cried. "Kill them at once!"

What a fool I'd been! I'd ignored the clues of the meadow. I had eaten the rabbit without questioning where it came from.

I scrambled away from the ruddy male, making a dash for a cluster of nettles and the open grass that lay beyond. Forepaws smacked against my back and teeth bore down on my neck.

Haiki was yelping somewhere behind me. "Stop! You've got it wrong!"

"Shut him up, before he brings others!"

"Into the den! We'll deal with them there."

A sprig of grass was teasing me, tickling my nose on the gentle breeze. Its fresh, sweet smell promised freedom and life. The life I'd given up. All for a rest, and some mouthfuls of rabbit.

I snapped at the stem so it tore between my teeth; tasted grass as they pulled me down.

Down into the dark.

6

A memory. One morning, long ago, I came up from the warmth of the den and blinked into the light. My whiskers tingled with cold as I peered across our patch. The sky was pigeon-feather gray, and the ground was dusted in glittering frost. Beyond it, the grass blades looked rigid as twigs.

My eyes widened. "Pirie, look!" Everything sparkled.

He shuffled alongside me, sniffing and yipping.

Greatma brushed past us, treading lightly on the crisp white grass. She turned to lick our noses.

"It's too cold for you to play, cubs. Stay inside. Your ma and fa are hunting. It's hard to find prey beneath the frost. I need to do what I can."

My ears pricked up. "Can't we come too?"

Pirie's tail gave a hopeful wag. "We could help to dig."

He started bouncing up and down and I copied him, kicking up chips of sparkling earth.

"No, cubs, you need to stay where it's warm and safe. Don't leave the den. I won't be long." Greatma gave us a sharp look and we backed inside, our tails drooping. She prowled over the frost toward the wildway. We craned our necks, taking in the white world of our patch. When Greatma reached the fence, she whipped around. "Get inside! Right now!"

We scrambled deeper into the den, dipping our heads beneath roots that bowed above the soil. It was warmer there, shielded from the wind. I curled up with a sigh. I could hear Greatma's paws as they crunched over the frost, growing fainter.

"Isla, what are you doing?" Pirie was watching me, head cocked.

"What do you think? Waiting for Greatma."

His tail gave a mischievous wag. "I think it's going to snow. Don't you want to see? That's when little white mice fall down from the clouds."

I raised my muzzle proudly. "I know what snow is! I've seen it before."

He butted me with his muzzle. "No, you haven't!"

I nipped his tail. "Have too!"

He shook me off and started padding away. "Then you won't want to see it again." I watched him clamber up the entrance, his back paw scrabbling against a root. With a kick he was out of the den, his tail-tip quivering with excitement.

"Wait for me!" I hurried to join him.

We crunched over the frost. I felt a chill in my paw pads and a shiver down my back. The icy air coated everything silvery white. Scents vanished beneath its shimmering pelt.

"Look at this!" Pirie drew in gulps of breath. When he released them, small clouds of mist bloomed in front of his snout. I stared as they hovered before him on the air. I breathed in deeply and puffed out mist through my nose. Two thin curls climbed lazily above my head. Pirie dived at them, snapping his teeth.

My tail thumped in amusement. Then I looked beyond the mist and my ears flattened. "Where's the sun?" I couldn't see it in the gray sky.

Pirie paused in thought. "Maybe the sun hides when it's really cold like today."

"But Fa said the sun rises every day. That means cold days too."

"Well, it isn't up there now, is it?"

I struggled over the frozen grass, my paws skidding against the brittle stems. "I guess not . . ." I noticed a narrow gap in the fence at the side of our patch. I hadn't been this far from the den before. A guilty flutter caught my tail and I gave myself a shake. I glanced over my shoulder. The den was still in view—that meant it was all right. I padded toward the gap in the fence that led to the neighboring patch. My eyes widened. Something glittered among short blades of frosted grass. A huge, flat, silvery circle. A twinkle of color crossed over it, a hint of yellow and gold. I had to squint when I looked at the circle—the sparkle stung my eyes.

Pirie was by my side. "What is it?"

I lapped at my muzzle. "I'm not sure, but I think . . ." My eyes shot to the sky, then down to the brilliant circle. "I think the sun may be trapped down there."

I felt my paws advancing. I slid under the gap beneath the fence and squinted at the circle. Pirie scrambled behind me—I could sense the warmth of his fur. From the corner of my eye I saw his breath escape as tendrils of mist.

We weren't supposed to leave the patch alone. Greatma had warned us to stay in the den. But what if the sun was down there, beneath the ice? What if it was in trouble? Did that mean the frost would stay forever? I could feel it tingling over my back, sharpening my hairs to glinting points. Without the sun to warm the land, everything would freeze. The earth would grow hard; the mice would vanish. The sky would darken into endless night.

I turned to Pirie, my whiskers flexing.

"We have no choice," I told him gravely. "We have to rescue the sun."

*   *   *

The foxes shunted me down a tunnel that plunged under the earth. One strutted in front of me, the dark contour of her body barely visible among the shadows. Others snapped at my heels. I stumbled, gulping for breath. I could hear Haiki's whimpers behind me, and the scrabble of more paws along the tunnel. How many of them were there?

The fox in front of me entered the den. Starlight peeked between tiny gaps in the ceiling, the underbelly of a tree. It looked like a tangle of brown rats' tails. Whiskery roots hung over the den, dangling tiny clods of soil. I blinked, adapting to the darkness. The odor of warm fur reached my nose and my ears flattened in confusion. There was no hint of ash or cinder.

But there was nothing comforting in the hard stares that greeted me and Haiki as we backed against the wall of the den. Eight sets of eyes bored into us.

The fox who'd first seized on us—the one they called Flint—pressed ahead of the others, a growl revealing the tips of his fangs. In the half-light, the dark fur on his face made his eyes look like great black voids.

"They're going to kill us," Haiki said, nuzzling his head against my shoulder. I gulped, my body stiff.

Flint's teeth glinted. "Death is all you deserve, you filthy lice." The others spat in agreement.

A young, dark-furred fox stalked up to Flint's side. "Don't kill them right away. Ask them what they want!"

Another young fox appeared next to her. "Simmi's right." He slammed down a furious forepaw. "We should find out what they know about the Tailless Seer."

Haiki yelped but I gritted my teeth. I wouldn't make a sound. I squeezed my paw pads against the ground, willing my legs not to tremble. A pointy-faced vixen edged between the others. "Shall we start by gnawing the fur off their forelegs?" A pink tongue whipped menacingly over her muzzle. She took a step toward us. "Tell us, ghost-creatures—what is the Tailless Seer planning?"

Haiki was whining. "We don't know what you mean! We don't know any seer!"

I frowned. Why had the vixen mentioned our forelegs? I glanced at her legs but it was too dark to see any marks. I looked more closely at the foxes, examining their eyes. There was no sign of red, no gunk encrusted on their mouths.

What had the large fox said?

Slaves of the Tailless Seer.

They weren't the Taken: these foxes were bright-eyed and alert. Their fur smelled alive. Beneath their aggression I sensed real fear. My ears flicked forward. "They mean the Mage!"

Haiki didn't seem to hear me. "Please don't hurt us! We don't know anything!"

The large male hissed impatiently. "They're not going to talk."

66

"What are we going to do with them?" said the pointy-faced vixen, her muzzle contorting with disgust. "We can't keep them prisoner."

"We can't let them go!" barked the young male. "They'll run straight back to *him*. We'll never be safe!"

I leaped to my paws. "You've got it wrong!" The large fox called Flint hissed at me but I didn't recoil. I had to explain, and fast. "You think we're from the Mage's skulk—that we're slaves of—" What had they called him? "Of the 'Tailless Seer.' But we're not. We're normal, healthy . . . We were running from those foxes when we reached your meadow. That's why we were so hungry and tired. It's why we ate your food. We weren't thinking."

"Don't listen to her!" urged the young dark-furred fox. "It's a trick."

I locked eyes on the pointy-faced vixen. "Look at us. Do we *seem* like mindless slaves? You can tell we're like you, I know you can. Just like I can tell. We're running from the same threat." My eyes trailed over the other foxes. They blinked back at me in silence. Even Haiki settled down, his whimpers subsiding into sniffles.

The pointy-faced vixen made a sudden movement toward us. Haiki yelped and threw himself against the wall but I stood still, my ears flat against my head. She stared into my eyes and I stared back. Her gaze trailed over my foreleg. She sighed at length. "They aren't pleached."

It was as though all the foxes released their breaths at the same time. I saw the tension ease around their muzzles.

Flint dipped his head. "Karo is right. These are free foxes."

The dark young vixen glowered. "So what are they doing here?"

I turned to face her. "I told you, we ran from the Taken—what you call 'pleached foxes.' We were crossing the Wildlands and came to a strange place, where the grass is dead and the air smells rank. That's where they found us."

"The Ghost Valley," murmured the young male. The other foxes exchanged nervous glances.

"Then there was . . . this burst of yelps that broke into a screech. A beast, something larger than a fox I think." I stiffened at the memory.

The sharp-snouted vixen, the one they called Karo, tapped her brush on the floor of the den. When she spoke there was a growl in her voice. "Could be a coyote. There's a pack that hunts beyond the lake, though I've never known them to cross into the Ghost Valley."

"I'm not sure," I admitted, never having heard of a coyote. "But the Taken raced after it. We managed to escape but we were so tired." I shook my head.

Karo glanced at Flint, then back at me. "You've obviously never seen a coyote. Pleached foxes wouldn't have chased one. They're dangerous."

"Did the skulk have a leader?" Flint cut in. "Did you notice a free fox among them, one that wasn't pleached?"

Again that strange term. *Pleached*. Bristling, I thought of Karka, the one-eyed vixen who had led the attack on my family. I remembered what Siffrin had said about her—that she too was a servant to the Mage.

. . . But unlike Tarr and the others, she does his bidding freely.

She hadn't been one of the Taken.

When I thought of the foxes who'd chased us in the valley, I pictured dead, red-rimmed eyes.

"I don't think so."

Karo leaned over to Flint. "She says they chased a coyote. Why would they do that?"

The dark-faced fox was examining me. "She probably got it wrong. She's only a cub."

"Born so long before malinta?"

"Must have been."

They looked at me searchingly. I knew what they meant—that I was born before day and night were equal length, before the buds unfurled in the trees. That there was something strange about me.

The vixen spoke. "Where are your parents, Cub? Where is your skulk?"

They'd probably know if I lied. "I'm from the Graylands. The Mage, the one you call the Tailless Seer . . . he sent his skulk to kill my family. I got away and so did my brother. He's lost somewhere in the Wildlands. I'm going to find him." My voice snagged on the knot of rage that lived in the pit of my belly.

Karo's ears twisted forward. "And your friend?" She gave Haiki a vaguely disapproving look.

His voice quavered. "I met Isla in the Wildlands. We're the same, me and her. The Mage stole my family."

"You're from the Graylands too?"

"I'm from the Lower Wildlands." He glanced at me, then back to the long-snouted vixen.

"The Tailless Seer took your family away?"

Haiki spoke in a quiet, determined voice. "I wasn't there, but I *know* it was him, or members of his skulk. Other skulks have disappeared. They weren't the first. But I have a plan."

The vixen tilted her head curiously. "What sort of plan?"

Haiki lowered his gaze. "I'm going to find the Elders. I'm going to get their help."

The vixen's eyes widened. She exchanged a quick look with Flint.

Flint took a step forward so he was level with Karo. "You shouldn't have stolen our food."

"I'm sorry," Haiki whimpered. "That was my fault. Isla had nothing to do with it."

I was grateful for his loyalty, but I was just as much to blame. "I ate the rabbit too," I pointed out.

70

"I found it," Haiki insisted. "I should have realized it was a skulk's cache. Sometimes I don't think . . ." He looked to Flint and Karo, wide-eyed, his tail giving a sudden unexpected wag. "We can catch you another rabbit! Or . . . or two rabbits, three!"

Haiki was going too far, making promises we couldn't keep. "You're right," I cut in. "We shouldn't have taken your cache. Hunger makes you do reckless things." I looked along the wall of foxes who were still blocking our way out of the den. A pang of irritation touched my whiskers. "We didn't mean any harm. Maybe I hoped the Wildlands would be friendlier than the Graylands. I guess I got that wrong."

"Isla!" hissed Haiki, flashing me a warning look.

"That's not much of an apology," Flint pointed out.

I stood stiffly, unwilling to say any more. These foxes had bullied and shunted us, had threatened us with death. Now that they knew we weren't the Taken, they should let us go. My head was thumping. I wasn't going to beg for forgiveness.

The vixen lowered herself to a sitting position. "We've heard of other foxes disappearing."

Flint spoke sharply. "Karo, you don't know that we can trust them."

Her ears rotated and she held my gaze. "We can, though, can't we?"

I dipped my head in acknowledgment.

Karo continued. "There's a small heath before you reach our patch. It neighbors the Ghost Valley. A skulk lived there, our cousins. But there's no trace of them now."

"One of our foxes has gone too," said the young male quietly. "Liro, Ma's brother. He was out one night and never came back. He was the fastest fox in the skulk and as good a hunter as Ma."

"That could have been anything," the dark-furred vixen pointed out. "An accident . . . the furless."

Karo's slim red tail gave a jerk. "He was always so sharp-witted. The last fox you'd ever imagine to be caught in a furless trap."

I cleared my throat. "Is the Ghost Valley where the Taken live?"

She tipped her head. "The pleached foxes? No, not there. They lurk in the forest beyond it and roam the valley by night. For a long time it just lay there, festering. Not anymore. The valley is growing, bleeding into our lands. We weren't always this nervous," she added, almost apologetic. "We're no longer safe in our own den."

A scruffy old fox settled down along the edge of the den. "Don't start that again, Karo. We're not going anywhere. This is our patch. We can't just run—we have to defend it."

"Defend it how?" she replied.

Flint's tail thumped the ground. "Day and night draw even, it's almost malinta. With more maa, we can fight them!"

Karo's ears rotated. "We're outnumbered, we don't stand a chance."

The skulk started talking over one another, yapping anxiously, as though we weren't there.

"I can fight!" yelped the dark-furred female, slashing an invisible adversary with her claws.

The young male gnashed his teeth. "I'll fight too!"

Karo's nose twitched on her pointed face. "How are we supposed to take on so many pleached foxes?"

"Foxcraft!" yipped the dark-furred male.

"We don't know any," Karo pointed out.

"The *Elders* know foxcraft," said Haiki.

One by one, the skulk fell silent, turning to look at him with new interest.

"The Elders know," echoed the small male, rising to his paws. There was a crook in his tail and a gray smudge on one side of his muzzle. "They can make themselves invisible, or sound like other creatures. I've heard they can even change their shape. Is that true?"

"Who cares if it's true?" the old fox growled irritably. "We don't have anything to do with *them*."

"They've never done us any good whatsoever," agreed Flint.

"Keep to themselves," said Karo. "Look down on ordinary skulks."

"But they're keepers of foxlore—they know *everything*," said Haiki in a voice of hushed awe.

My tail twitched as I remembered Siffrin's praise for Jana. "I don't need the Elders."

The old fox snorted. "Just as well. Do you think they'd be ready to share their knowledge with a Graylands cub and a dumpy fox from the lowlands?"

Haiki flinched but he spoke up, his voice trembling. "You can say what you like about me. I know I'm nothing special. And it's my fault that we ate your cache . . . But don't underestimate Isla." He gave me a reassuring blink.

"Your devotion to the cub is admirable," said the old fox coolly. "Don't expect such loyalty from the Elders. They won't even help their sisters and brothers from the Upper Wildlands." The old fox's eyes flashed. "I've lived in this meadow since I was a cub, since before the Ghost Valley even existed. There were ferns there once, and hazel groves, and a pond where ducks clacked, easy prey. I've watched it rot. The hazels decayed. The ducks flew away and the pond sank into the mud." His voice rose angrily. "In its place, there are noxious mushrooms and red-eyed foxes in endless numbers. They terrorize our meadows. They threaten our skulks." He snorted through his nose. "And you from the lowlands, you seek the Elders."

Haiki dipped his head but the old fox wasn't finished. "They must know what's happening in our world. Yet they will not share their most precious gift—but for the chosen few, they will not teach us wa'akkir."

A shiver ran along my back, down to the tip of my brush. *The shape-shifting foxcraft.* I had watched Siffrin change his appearance in moments, had seen Karka, the Mage's assassin, turn into a giant dog. I understood the power of wa'akkir.

The old fox took in Haiki through narrowed eyes. "What makes you think you can find the Elder Rock? More experienced foxes have tried and failed. You are strangers to our land."

"Fa," urged Karo, stepping toward the old fox, but she stopped when she saw the look in his eyes.

"I won't be silenced!" he spat. "This foolish gray should know what he's up against." He turned back to Haiki. "Even if you managed it, by some incredible luck—even if you crossed the shana to reach the Elder Rock—you would never gain the help you seek. You'd have wasted your time on some dangerous quest and you'd still be left without wisdom or aid. Do not be deceived into thinking the Elders care. Death and decay, yet they keep to themselves. They do nothing."

The old fox rose shakily to his paws, turned, and started out of the den. His long brush was skinny and patchy in places. It dragged on the earth as he walked. His voice faded as he padded away. "Do not seek foxlore as an answer to your problems. The Elders would sooner die than share its secrets."

7

The old fox shambled along the tunnel.

I edged to Haiki's side. "Let's get out of here."

We started toward the exit. Karo and Flint stepped back to let us pass.

The dark-furred vixen was less obliging. "So they walk free? Just like that? They ate the rabbit, Ma, the one you caught yesterday!"

Karo sighed. "They were hungry and tired. They'd been chased by pleached foxes."

I paused and Haiki shuffled close to me. "What are you doing?" he mumbled. "They're letting us go."

My ears twisted. It was the term the vixen had used. "Pleached." My attention was fixed on Karo and Flint. "You mean the Taken? The Mage's skulk?"

Flint didn't look so scary anymore. Now that my sight

had adapted to the darkness, the patches on his face no longer made his eyes ghoulishly large. "We call them 'pleached' because of what's been done to them."

"By the Mage?"

"Yes, if you mean the Tailless Seer . . . or at least by the Narral, his inner guard."

"Who are they?"

"Isla . . ." Haiki nudged me, his eyes wide. "We should get out of here while we can." But I didn't feel threatened by this skulk anymore. Above everything else, I yearned for answers.

Flint dropped his gaze. "The ones you speak of as 'the Taken,' they were ordinary foxes once. But now they're pleached. They're the Seer's slaves. Their wills have been sucked from their bodies."

I already knew that, but hearing it again made me picture those blank eyes. For the first time I wondered how it worked. How was the will extracted from a living fox? "Is pleaching . . . is it a foxcraft?"

"Of a kind." Karo lowered her voice. "We do not know how it is done. Some say there must be flames."

"I don't believe it," said one of the old vixens. "Foxes do not burn their gifts."

Flint's head snapped up and his ears flicked back. "Rupus loathes the Elders for hoarding the secrets of foxlore. But they are not alone in their command of foxcraft. The Tailless Seer knows it all too well."

His words weighed heavily on me. I'd thought that fox-craft was a *good* thing, that it protected our kind from the furless. But if it could be used by one fox to control another . . .

"*Isla!*" Haiki's whine had grown urgent.

I started forward again, slipping between Flint and Karo toward the narrow tunnel. "I'm sorry about the rabbit," I murmured.

Karo called after me. "Go safely, Cub." The other foxes watched in silence.

"That was close," whispered Haiki when we were out of earshot of the others and climbing up the tunnel.

"I don't think they'd have hurt us. They thought we were the Taken—*pleached*. They were just trying to scare us. They're scared themselves, you can sense it—terrified of the Mage and his skulk."

"They called him the Tailless Seer," Haiki pointed out.

"But they meant the same fox."

"Do you really think he hasn't got a tail?" Haiki asked.

Instinctively, my own brush swept close to my flank.

His strange, pale eyes, that shrub of a tail.

The answer came from above us at the mouth of the tunnel. "That is what they say." The voice was cracked with age. It was the old fox who'd cursed the Elders and left the den in disgust. As I padded along the tunnel, I saw him come into view.

He spoke without looking at us. "How the Seer lost his tail is a matter of endless speculation. Perhaps he was born that way. Some will tell you it was torn off in a fight with a wolf, but wolves haven't lived this far south since the age of the furless began. Others claim it was severed in an accident. Then there are those who say he chewed it off himself, to prove pain doesn't frighten him." When I caught the green shimmer of the old fox's eyes, my confidence melted. "They said we could go." I was ashamed by the mewl in my voice.

The old fox eyed me as I leveled alongside him by the entrance to the den. He wasn't much taller than I was. Perhaps he had shrunk with age. "You are free to do what you choose. If that is to leave, don't let me stop you."

Was there a threat beneath his words?

Haiki was already scrambling past the old fox, climbing out of the den and stretching in the nettles. My snout drank in the night air and my ears grasped for sounds. I smelled earth, grass, wood bark. I heard wind, crickets . . . and something else. Far away, hard to disentangle . . . I strained my ears but the sound sank from my reach.

I stood quite still. Then I caught it: a distant stutter of gekkers.

The fur was sharp along my back.

The old fox eyed me knowingly. "Pleached foxes," he confirmed. "Could it be that they're looking for you?"

My tail-tip quivered. How had he guessed? "You said they stalked the Wildlands at night. Why should it be anything to do with me?"

"I sense it," he said. "You sense it too. Is that why they sought you out in the Graylands? I've never known pleached foxes to travel so far from their master's lair."

"They came for my brother."

The old fox stared at me until I broke away, unable to hold his gaze. When he spoke again, his voice was soft. "Do you wish to take your chances on the night? Wouldn't you rather be safe in the den?" I glanced at him and his eyes glittered. I saw warmth I hadn't noticed before.

He turned and padded back along the tunnel, his patchy tail trailing behind him. I heard another stutter of gekkers, still distant yet drawing closer. Had the Taken crossed the valley? Had they reached the outskirts of the meadow?

"Haiki," I called softly. "We'll have to stay here tonight. It isn't safe in the meadow."

His broad gray face appeared between the nettles. "Go back in *there*? But those foxes are dangerous, Isla. They were going to kill us! Don't tell me you trust them all of a sudden?"

"The Mage's skulk is roaming. We'll have to wait it out until morning." My muzzle tensed. "It has nothing to do with trust," I added. "I don't trust anyone."

As I turned back toward the den, I caught a glimpse of Haiki's face. He winced, his shoulders drooping. A guilty prickle touched my whiskers.

The scene that greeted us was very different from the one we'd left. Instead of standing up, backs arched, the foxes were reclining along a wall of the den.

The old fox must have told the skulk about the Taken; they didn't seem surprised to see us again. Karo and Flint were grooming each other. The young male was swatting the female's tail. She flipped on her back and gave him a kick. The smaller male was stretched out on his belly, lapping his gray-smudged muzzle. Two mature females looked up mildly as we entered.

The old fox sat apart from the others. "Simmi, Tao, go to the front and rear exits. If pleached foxes are prowling, we should be on guard."

The young male paused, his paw suspended over the female's tail. "They'll never find us down here."

"Oh, won't they?" The old fox glared. "Do you want to wait and see if you're right?"

The two young foxes rose grudgingly. The male stalked to an exit at the edge of the den that I hadn't noticed before. The female padded past me and Haiki but scarcely gave us a second look. I could hear her paws against the earth as she wove her way along the tunnel.

The old fox turned to us. "Since you're staying the night, and you've already enjoyed Karo's prey, perhaps it's time for proper introductions. I'll start things off. My name is Rupus. I was born in this meadow, a little upstream. I'm older than anyone else around here. I'm probably as old as that stone mountain you'll have crossed if you came from the lowlands."

Karo rolled onto her side. "I'm Rupus's daughter, Karo. This is my mate, Flint." She nodded at the dark-faced male. "Simmi and Tao, who just left, are our cubs from last malinta, as is Mox." She leaned over to the small male and gave him a lick on the nose.

"We're Karo's aunts," said one of the mature vixens. "Dexa and Mips."

"No one around here is as old as I am," Rupus muttered. He turned to us, his face grizzled. "What about you? You tell us you have both suffered under the Tailless Seer. We know that one of you, at least, is foolish enough to seek the aid of the Elders. What else?"

Haiki quailed from the attention of the skulk. My tail jerked uneasily. I had already said too much. I gathered the memory of Pirie close to my heart. I wasn't about to share it with strangers. "What do you want to know?"

"You could start by telling us your names."

*   *   *

Shards of light broke through the lattice of roots overhead. The skulk slept in a heap along the wall of the den, heads nestled on flanks and long brushes sweeping around one another. Even the grizzled Rupus rested his muzzle by Karo's belly.

I blinked away the fug of my dreamless sleep. Gazing up at the pale morning light, I thought of Pirie, remembering the carefree nights we had curled up side by side. Where was he now? When I'd searched for him in the Snarl, strange flashes of knowledge had come to me unbidden. I'd pictured him at a huge stone furless—seen flickers of graystone through Pirie's eyes.

I had reached him through gerra-sharm.

But now, though I sensed that my brother was in the Wildlands—that he was closer than ever—it was harder to detect him. When I reached out my thoughts, I felt him retreat. Was he avoiding me?

I looked around the den at the sleeping foxes. This wasn't my skulk. It wasn't my home.

I didn't have a home anymore.

I needed to find somewhere quiet so I could reach out to Pirie through gerra-sharm. I'd let Haiki know I was leaving, that from here I'd be traveling alone. I owed him that much at least. We had run from the hunter together, and had escaped from the Taken. But as my eyes trailed over the den, I realized that Haiki wasn't there.

A shrill howl pierced the stillness of the morning. I knew at once that it wasn't a fox. It was the same strange cry I'd heard in the Ghost Valley. The skulk sprang to life, alert and wild-eyed. I felt their panic fan around me as the voice was joined by others. Shrill cries tore across the meadow.

"Coyotes," gasped Karo. "They must be close."

Rupus's face darkened. "Closer than they've ever come before."

I'd only heard one in the valley. "They move in packs?"

"Sometimes," said Flint, hurrying past me. His claws scrabbled along the tunnel. He must have been joined by Tao, the young male on guard. I could hear them murmuring to each other. Soon they retreated into the den.

The young female, Simmi, appeared from the other tunnel. "It sounds like a coyote is right outside."

Flint spoke softly. "He's circling the den." He cast a wary glance at Karo. "They've been known to steal newborns, but there aren't any small cubs here. I can't imagine what they want . . ."

Karo drew in her breath. "We should wait it out until they pass."

"You're right," said Flint. "The sun isn't fully up yet. Between coyotes and pleached foxes, we're better off down here. It's almost dawn. At least the pleached foxes will run for the forest as soon as the light comes up."

Rupus was solemn. "I pity any fox roaming the meadow."

I rose to my paws. "Haiki's out there."

Rupus clicked his tongue. "Poor dumb creature. I doubt you'll be seeing him again."

Friendly, talkative Haiki . . . All he wanted was his family back.

I took a step toward the exit. "I'm going to look for him."

Karo moved to block my path. "I'm afraid I can't allow that. The coyotes or pleached foxes may find you, and you'd lead them straight to us. There's nothing you can do for your friend. There is only hope. Hope that Canista's Lights will show him a path."

I opened my mouth to protest but a piercing howl scorched the words from my tongue. Fear skittered over my pelt. It must have been a coyote, and yet . . . I felt sure I knew that voice. Then the cry took shape as a single word, over and over like a chant.

"Isla. Isla. Isla."

Karo's jaw fell open and she gazed overhead, squinting at the light between the roots. In that moment I shot past her and out of the tunnel.

A low mist was swirling over the meadow, touched with the first pink flush of dawn. He towered above the nettles on slender legs. His nose was black, his muzzle creamy, and one of his ears was torn at the end. A jagged scar above his lip sent his whiskers out at an angle.

He reminded me of Farraclaw, the wolf from the beast

dens. The coyote was smaller, leaner, but he was still twice the size of a fox. There was power in his slim legs and the set of his muscular jaw.

A rich smell drifted on the breeze. The coyote's eyes rested on mine. Deep within that golden gaze, there was something knowing.

My belly flipped.

Siffrin.

"Isla, at last . . ." He took a small step toward me, hopeful and strangely shy. "I thought I'd never find you."

8

Siffrin was in wa'akkir, in the shape of a coyote. His bushy coat was sandy and his short thick tail swished in the breeze.

My fur tingled, my tail leaping up uncertainly.

He protected me from the Taken. But he lied about my family.

I felt footfalls from the den. Karo, Flint, Tao, and Simmi climbed out of the exit. Flint's hackles were raised. "What are you doing here, Coyote? This is fox land. We want no trouble from your kind."

The coyote's gaze lingered on me, then shifted to Flint. "And you'll get none."

Karo arched her back. "You've already been told, get away! And take the rest of your pack."

"I don't have a pack."

"We heard them," Karo hissed. "Coyotes howling together."

I cleared my throat. "It isn't what you think . . ."

Simmi was sniffing, her ears pinned back. "There's something strange about him, Ma."

Siffrin looked at me as though the others weren't there. "You guessed it was me? Even though I karakked?"

My ears swiveled forward and my paw rose, but I didn't move any closer. "I knew your voice."

Siffrin lowered his muzzle. "I've searched for you since I lost you to the snatchers."

I held his gaze, my paw still hovering in front of me.

"I never meant to lie to you, Isla."

My eyes trailed to Siffrin's foreleg, but the mark of the broken rose was disguised in wa'akkir. He cocked his head, his expression fading from hope to regret.

Tao, the young male, was sniffing deeply. "I thought you said you didn't have a pack?"

Siffrin's eyes widened and his ears rotated.

Then I heard it—the chorus of yaps. A group of coyotes emerged from the mist. Their eyes skated over the foxes at the entrance to the den. They couldn't see Siffrin behind thick shrubs.

Karo, Flint, Tao, and Simmi arched their backs as the coyotes approached. A large, pale-furred female headed the pack.

"Come no further!" Karo spat bravely. "We don't want to fight you, but we will if we have to."

The coyote snorted. "You? Fight us?" The rest of the pack yipped in amusement. Her yellow eyes darkened. "You'll be forced to if you don't give us the rabbits. We came to see this land of plenty with our own eyes. We have traveled far this night. Do not disappoint us, Fox." The coyote scratched the earth with her long claws.

"There are scarcely enough rabbits in this meadow to feed our skulk," hissed Flint. "Our cache is empty. We cannot help you."

My tail twitched guiltily.

The coyote sniffed, her eyes sliding over the foxes and across the tangling grass. "I smell no abundance of rabbits." Her lip peeled back and she growled in frustration. "We are deceived!"

"Sneaky foxes!" snarled the pack. "Wicked foxes!" They started forward, snarling and yapping, spit bubbling at their jaws.

Siffrin whispered to me urgently. "I was traveling alone . . ." His ears were flat. "Isla, you must know how hard I tried to find you. I'll lead this pack away—I won't let them hurt you."

I didn't have time to answer. He stepped out from between the shrubs to face the coyotes. "Leave the foxes alone."

The coyotes fell back in confusion, their cackles lapsing into whines.

"Chief!" spluttered the pale-furred female. "I thought you would want us to . . ." Her words trailed away. I could see her nostrils pulsing. "You smell . . . different."

"*Different?*" snarled Siffrin, rising to his full height and glaring at the pack.

"I am mistaken, Chief," she whined, collapsing before him and exposing her creamy belly. "I beg your forgiveness."

The pack started to dip their heads and fawn, backing away with muzzles lowered.

They're scared of Siffrin!

He had shifted his shape into a coyote, but not just any coyote: the chief of the pack. I watched in amazement as they whimpered their apologies. From the reaction of the pack, I guessed the real chief was formidable.

"There is nothing here for us," Siffrin sniffed. "Ground squirrels live at the foot of the hills. Let's go."

The pack muttered and yelped in agreement.

An outraged howl cut over their voices. "How dare you scrape and pander to another? I am your leader! I am your chief!" A figure shoved between the coyotes and they dropped to the ground, whining and rolling, kicking their paws in the air. The chief strode toward Siffrin. His head was raised proudly and contempt was etched onto his muzzle. One of his long, pointed ears was torn at the end. There was a jagged scar above his lip.

Standing behind me, Simmi gasped. "Those two coyotes . . . they're just the same!"

It was the leader of the pack: the one that Siffrin was imitating. With a lurch I remembered the dread I'd felt on seeing myself as an echo in wa'akkir. That was Siffrin in disguise, too. *I might have killed him . . .*

The coyote chief locked eyes on his double as his pack tossed and whimpered around him. At first I saw confusion on his face.

It was quickly replaced by rage. "What *are* you?" he choked. "How *dare* you?"

I glanced at Karo and the other foxes. They stared, bewildered, at the two chiefs standing off.

"Siffrin, what are you doing?" I hissed. "Don't you remember how dangerous this is? You'll send him mad!"

Siffrin kept his attention on the chief but murmured to me in a low voice. "This is my fault, Isla. I thought the coyotes were far behind me, but I must have led them to this den. It's my mistake and I'll fix it." He started stalking away from me, his attention on the coyote chief.

"I don't get it!" Tao whined.

"How is this possible?" breathed Simmi in awe.

"Foxcraft," I murmured as Siffrin edged into the deep foliage.

The chief exploded into frightful yelps. "You! What *are* you? *Who are you?*" He spat on the ground and stumbled, belching noisily. "You trickster. You . . . monster!" He lurched at Siffrin's disappearing tail. "I'll get you," he snarled. "I'll *kill* you!" He burst forward and Siffrin sprang out of the way, breaking across the meadow. The coyote staggered into a run, clumsy but determined, and the baffled pack started after him.

"The first coyote knew Isla," said Tao. "He called her by her name."

The foxes fell silent. I felt their eyes boring into my back. But I didn't turn, I was already running—chasing the pack into the morning mist.

The coyotes were pounding through the grass, their tails bobbing in formation. I hurried behind them as they zig-zagged between hazel and pointy gorse with yellow flowers. They stormed toward the rising sun, their fur dusted gold in the morning light. Siffrin and the chief were already far ahead, beyond my range of vision.

The stream appeared, tumbling into my path. I ran alongside it, lagging behind the coyotes. Everything was different in the light of dawn. The chirping night creatures had retreated, replaced by buzzing insects. A rabbit was hopping near the base of a tree. I didn't spare it a second glance.

The land staggered uphill and the stream fell away, the

ground growing grainy beneath my paws. Ferns sprang up along the meadow, crowding a path toward tall pines. I was falling behind the coyotes, who ran with impressive endurance and speed. Panting wildly, I saw them dive over the ferns and duck beneath the trees.

By the time I entered the forest, I could hardly see the pack, but I could hear their yelps and heavy breaths and feel their footfalls as they thumped the loam. Up rose the ground beneath my paws, climbing sharply into a hill. Pain pulsed in my legs and my muscles quivered but I pushed on harder, determined to catch up with them.

As I dived between two trees, I stumbled on a knotty root. My legs folded under me and I fell onto the spongy forest floor, my chest heaving.

With a grimace, I dragged myself upright and started loping more slowly among the pines. It was no use. I could no longer feel the vibration of thumping paws. Had the coyotes finally stopped, or were they too far away to detect? My ears rotated and my whiskers edged forward. As I bounded down the hump of the hill I heard yelps and growls. I saw the edges of a rocky plain and the outline of furry bodies. They were springing up and down, snarling and baying in a circle like dogs.

Two figures fought in the middle.

Siffrin was confronting the chief. I stalked closer, hanging behind the trees. The sight was disturbing: two identical coyotes facing off. I couldn't make out which one was Siffrin. I watched tensely as they jostled and snapped, rolling together and breaking apart.

"Filthy impostor!" One of the coyotes lunged at the other, throwing him onto his back. The one who fell—it must have been Siffrin—cried out as he smacked the stone ground. Not far from where he landed, the rocky plane ended abruptly. From my angle at the edge of the trees, I couldn't see what stood beyond.

The pack closed in around the warring coyotes, their bloodlust whipping them into howls. Occasionally they snapped at Siffrin, landing cruel bites on his flank, though they dropped back to let their chief do the fighting. It struck me that I was in terrible danger. If they turned, if they saw me, they'd kill me in their frenzy.

I cowered close to the base of a tree, trying to work out who was winning. I saw the fight in glimpses of fur within the baying pack. One of the fighting coyotes was wounded. I caught a flash of bright red blood.

Please don't let it be Siffrin.

The bloody coyote twisted away, panting heavily. "I don't want to fight. Let me go."

My heart sank. I knew that voice.

"You're not going anywhere!" spat the chief. Blood seeped from the edge of his mouth. I remembered the fury that had stolen my thoughts when I'd met Siffrin as my double. I knew that the chief would never give up. It was a kind of sickness of the mind. A coyote was powerful, more resilient than a fox cub. His pack roared him on as the haze of wa'akkir cast a spell of rage over him. He fell back onto his haunches. His powerful rear legs flexed as he prepared to pounce. He threw his jaws open and charged at Siffrin.

I held my breath.

At the last moment, Siffrin rolled out of the way, tumbling to a halt and scrambling to his paws. But the chief wasn't quick enough to stop. He flung himself forward, his legs pumping wildly as he flew over the rocky plain. I couldn't see how far he fell but I could tell that the chief was in trouble from the hushed whimpers of his pack.

They ran back and forth along the edge of the rock, whining and smacking into one another.

The pale coyote who'd threatened the fox skulk drew back and looked to the sky. "A blood sun is risen!" she howled in despair. "Our chief is dying!"

The pack dropped onto their bellies, yelping in terror and remorse.

"To the territory!" cried the pale coyote. "We must share our rites with the spirits."

The pack moved abruptly, their shrill howls rising in unison. I dropped into the undergrowth as they pounded past. I waited until I could no longer feel their pawsteps and their cries had faded on the breeze. Then I drew in my breath and stepped out from behind the tree.

I moved warily to the rock plane. Splatters of blood lit the sun-touched stone. With a deep breath, I peered over the edge. Brush-lengths down was another heel of rock, white and flat like a bone. On it lay the broken chief. He wasn't dead—or not yet. I heard his labored breath and saw his eyes reel in their sockets. A wave of sympathy broke inside me. I knew what it was to feel the sickness he'd felt. The rage, the violence . . . A coyote was a natural enemy, a threat to foxes. But the way things had ended . . . it wasn't all his fault.

His eyes rolled up in my direction but they seemed to gaze through me, to the sky beyond. They were wet and shiny like ice. What did he see up there? I glanced over my shoulder at the dawn light. It glowed deep crimson.

A blood sun is risen!

I shrank away from the edge of the rock and looked around me. At first I saw no sign of Siffrin. Then I heard a whimper. He had made it over the rock and into the woods, but he hadn't gone far. Under the shade of a giant fern, I saw him shudder and collapse on his side. He was still in the form of the coyote chief.

I ran to him. His eyes were squeezed shut and his breath escaped in shallow pants.

"What's wrong? Where does it hurt?" Urgently I sniffed his fur, examining his injuries. Blood gushed from scratches on his shoulders, and his flanks were riddled with bites, but none of these seemed deep. I found no sign of serious harm— nothing to explain his wretched state.

I thought of the real coyote chief, battered and broken on the rock below. Could it be that fox and coyote were somehow intertwined? What if the chief's death meant Siffrin's own?

Heat pulsed at my ears and my body ached with tension. "Change back!" I yelped. "You're still in wa'akkir. Change back to a fox, before it's too late!"

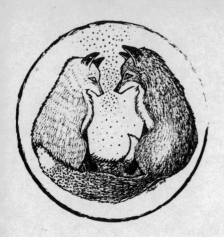

9

The sun cut a path between leafless branches, lighting up the forest floor. Birds warbled overhead, indifferent to Siffrin's suffering. His legs had started twitching and his eyes were still clamped shut.

"Listen to me," I snapped in frustration. "You have to change back!"

Paws crunched on twigs and I shot around to see a long, pointed snout. "Karo . . . What are you doing here?"

Flint, Simmi, and Tao appeared.

Haiki jogged up behind them, staring dumbly at me and Siffrin. "Isla, what's going on? I stepped out of the den for air and when I returned they said you'd run after a pack of coyotes?" His tail flicked anxiously. "I was so worried about you!"

"We were all worried," said Flint. "You're just a cub. We

saw the rest of the pack charging through the forest. They were making a terrible noise, howling and yelping."

"What happened to the coyote?" Simmi murmured. "There's something about him . . ."

Karo padded closer. "He isn't a coyote." She met my eye. "Is he, Isla?"

My whiskers bristled. "He's called Siffrin. He's trapped in wa'akkir."

"What do you mean?" asked Tao.

I didn't have time for this. "The shape-shifting foxcraft," I snapped. "He only *looks* like a coyote—like the coyote chief."

The young fox screwed up his muzzle. "All that jabber Mox came out with, about invisibility and changing shape . . . It can't be true?"

Karo spoke over him. "Where's the real chief?"

My voice was sharp with panic. "Over on the rocks, he's badly injured. I don't know, but I think that if he dies—"

"Then the fox dies too?" Karo's ears flipped back.

A mewl escaped my throat and I swallowed. Desperation was clawing at me. "He's too weak to change back into his own form."

The foxes padded closer, peering down at Siffrin. He was hardly moving anymore. I thought of the coyote chief, out on the bone-white rock.

Karo stepped alongside me. "There's nothing you can do. He doesn't have long."

Flint sniffed Siffrin's muzzle. "Can you hear that? Like a hiss in the air. His maa is departing."

I stared at Siffrin, helpless. I thought I could just sense a fizzle, like the softest breath. A shimmer of light hung over him. Sorrow crept over my pelt. I shook my head sharply. What had Flint just said?

His maa is departing.

There *was* something I could do!

"Open your eyes!" I barked, dropping down to Siffrin's ear. "Open your eyes *right now*."

He murmured and turned his head, his eyes still shut.

I pressed down very close to him as the other foxes watched. "Listen to me, Siffrin, I can't help unless you look at me. Don't tell me you're ready to give up so soon. I thought I knew you better."

His whiskers flexed. I could see how hard he was working just to take in my words. Then his eyelashes fluttered.

I could feel the other foxes staring but I didn't look up. I focused on Siffrin as he opened his eyes. They held the same icy gleam of the coyote chief. I tried not to think of that broken beast, dying alone on the rock. Instead I recalled the maa-sharm chant.

"With my touch, I sense you; with my eyes, I heal you. By Canista's Lights, I share what I have; we are knit together and you are whole."

His eyes were only half-open. Would it work? I waited

for that magical feeling to rise inside me, but all I heard was the warbling of birds and Siffrin's labored breath.

I tried again. "With my touch, I sense you; with my eyes, I heal you . . ."

The coyote's broad sandy muzzle wrinkled with effort as Siffrin's eyes widened. He forced himself to look at me properly. I felt a sharp yank and stumbled closer, as though he had pulled me toward him. I steadied myself, my gaze fixed on his. Something was happening. My whiskers bristled and my brush swept behind me, tingling with heat. I felt a flash of light leap between us as the world around me grew vague.

With my touch, I sense you; with my eyes, I heal you . . .

Memories raced through my mind. I pictured Pirie prancing by my side, his mottled tail lashing as he mock bowed and rolled in the grass. I heard Ma's voice, and the thump of Fa's paws on soft earth. The scent of hazel and cedar pricked my nose and I sighed, brought back to another time. Greatma padded through the wildway, a pigeon in her jaws. Pirie bounded toward her and I ran after him, shunting him out of the way with a friendly nudge. We growled and yipped as she set down the limp bird. I sank in my teeth, tasting the plump flesh. Pirie bit into the pigeon's leg and we jostled for the carcass, ripping off meat in a whirr of gray feathers.

I shook my fur, the feathers spinning around me like a snowstorm. Between them I saw a valley where rabbits ran anxious loops. A vixen stalked between marshes, lowering her body and angling her head with expert precision. Her coat was of the deepest red I'd ever seen. Slowly, she curved around the edge of a marsh, then paused, her ears twisting forward and back, before starting to run. She seized on a rabbit and threw it down, snapping its neck with a shake.

Her golden eyes turned my way.

She caught it for me, I thought gratefully. A surge of happiness struck me, so powerful that I caught my breath.

The spinning gray pigeon feathers rose in the wind. They knotted and clotted like clouds. As the sky grew darker, the red-furred vixen seemed further away. Lost amid marshes, fading from sight. I paused, head cocked. The feathers were on the move again, crumbling to ash, swept on the morning wind. I saw a blood-red sun as it rose on the horizon. Day turned to night, and night to day. Clouds drifted and parted and leaves grew bronze before floating down from the trees. They shimmered on the forest floor, gilded with an amber gleam. Burnished leaves, the color of dawn. The color of Siffrin's eyes.

He was the first to blink, just as he had been when we'd shared maa in the Snarl. His jaw strained with effort and he squeezed his eyes shut. In the moment that his eyes closed, I felt a sharp wrench and tumbled backward with a sigh. My head sank down to the forest floor and I panted for breath. There was a metallic taste in my mouth. Pain burrowed beneath the soft fur of my ears and expanded across my head. A deep fatigue crept over my body.

My paw pads were icy. The warmth of maa-sharm was replaced by a lingering sorrow.

Lifting my throbbing head to the pine trees, I forced myself to remember where I was. I looked around. Haiki, Karo, and the others were staring, but not at me. I followed their awestruck gazes back to Siffrin. Where the sandy-furred coyote had lain, a red-furred fox stretched his legs. His ears were pricked, his long brush flecked with light. His golden eyes were luminous.

Siffrin rose to his paws like a new fox.

I awoke in a warm, dark burrow on my own. The ground was dry beneath my belly and my paws had lost their icy chill. Gingerly, I stretched. The pain in my head had dulled. I yawned and shook out my fur.

I could smell other foxes nearby and hear the murmur of their voices. I was in the same den I'd stayed in the previous night. For a moment I couldn't remember how I'd returned there.

Then it came back: the exhaustion that ran through my limbs. The huddle of questions, bright eyes boring into me—the Wildlands foxes enthralled by maa-sharm— amazed by the dying coyote who'd transformed into a healthy fox.

Scarcely awake, I'd loped between Karo and Haiki as the other foxes looked on curiously. Siffrin tried to talk to me but his words had seeped away like mist. How long had it taken me to cross the forest and round back to the valley?

How long had I been sleeping in this burrow?

I hadn't imagined that sharing my maa would make me so weak. Siffrin had offered me his maa when I was hurt in the Snarl. He'd been all right after, hadn't he? Through the fog of my memories, I remembered his labored movements. I'd seen him wince with strain as he'd hobbled over the gray-stone. He had slept all day without twitching a muscle and I'd envied him his rest.

I realized now he must have struggled to place one paw before another, that his heavy sleep betrayed exhaustion. Had he hidden his suffering from me?

I remembered what I'd said to him back in the Snarl.

It sounds dangerous, offering your life source like that.

What had he replied?

Only if you give too much . . .

I padded to the edge of the burrow. I could hear the rumble of a deep voice. It was the old fox, Rupus. I pressed closer, ears pricked.

"Karo and Flint told me what happened. You looked like a coyote in his death throes. Then the cub helped you and you turned into a fox."

"He was always a fox." It was Karo's voice. "He had shape-shifted."

"I said there was something strange about him, didn't I say that, Ma?" I recognized Simmi, the dark-furred foxling.

"You did," Karo agreed. "I could sense it too. And so could the coyotes, though they feared insulting their leader."

Rupus's husky voice cut in. "So that was just a disguise?"

"Yes," said Siffrin from the other side of the wall. My ears flipped back and a growl caught in my throat. I felt a strange mixture of anger and relief. Why had he come here? I hadn't wanted him to die, but that didn't mean I'd forgiven him. "I was nowhere near the pack when I shifted into the image of their leader. I thought it would be safer to travel in wa'akkir. It's always worked in the past."

I pressed closer to the exit.

Rupus was stern. "I see you are proud of your foxcraft, but you haven't the sense to use it sparingly. You led a whole pack of coyotes to our den."

Siffrin's voice was soft. "I was *so* careful. I shifted my shape far from their lands. I can't understand how they caught up with me."

"Yet you suspect something," pressed Karo. "I can tell. Out with it, young fox. If we are in danger, we deserve to know why."

Siffrin sighed. "These past nights, as I've traveled the Wildlands in the form of the coyote, I've been hounded by the Taken at every turn. They chased me at the edge of the rocky mountain. They stalked me across heathland. I have never heard of foxes chasing coyotes. You know the evil I speak of? Foxes in body, but not in spirit."

I could almost feel the fabric of the air shift on the other side of the burrow—almost taste the tension that clung to the earth.

"We know who you mean all too well. Pleached foxes. They haunt the Ghost Valley."

"Yes, *pleached*." Siffrin sounded surprised that the old fox knew the word. And maybe a little impressed. I heard him draw in a slow breath. "I saw the Taken chasing Isla and . . . her friend, at the edge of the valley. I called them away. I wanted to distract them long enough so that Isla could escape. The Taken seemed all too willing to chase me—their ferocity took me by surprise. Like they knew that I wasn't a real coyote. As though they'd been waiting for me."

Crouching in the burrow, I remembered the howl that had drawn the Taken away from me and Haiki. That was Siffrin?

Rupus spoke again. "And you believe there is some connection? That these ghoulish foxes and the coyotes were conspiring against you? Why would they do that?"

Siffrin paused a long time. My ears twisted, taking in the sounds from the far side of the burrow. I could hear the shuffle of paws as a fox changed position. Otherwise all was still.

Finally the red-furred fox spoke. "I'm a messenger of the Elders."

There was a drawing in of breath.

"Do the Elders really know everything?" It was Tao.

"Why is the Tailless Seer pleaching Wildlands foxes?" asked Simmi.

"The Elders don't care about us," snarled Flint. "You heard what Rupus said. The Elders are indifferent to our suffering."

Siffrin's voice rose passionately. "That isn't true. The Elders are good. They care for the plight of all foxes."

"If they're so capable, why don't they stop the Seer?" asked Karo.

Siffrin sighed. "The Mage has power of his own. He must be leaching it from somewhere. The Elders are strong, but they cannot defeat an army of Taken. His maa must be greater than any fox who's ever lived. All except the Black Fox."

Quiet fell through the den.

The next voice to speak sounded fearful and young. "Can't the Black Fox stop the Seer?" I thought it was the smaller brother of Simmi and Tao. What had they called him? Mox.

Siffrin spoke very quietly. "This is sensitive, you understand. Our enemies must not learn of it but . . . The Black Fox has gone, no one knows where."

"Would you care to explain what a messenger of these great and mysterious foxes is doing in our humble meadow?" Rupus didn't conceal the contempt in his voice.

"There is talk of a young fox from the Graylands— concern she may be caught by the Mage."

"Go on," pressed Rupus.

"The Elders feared for her. And it was my fault she was in danger, because I lost her in the Graylands. I offered to find her again."

I stepped out of the burrow, entering the main part of the den. Siffrin was near the exit, his red tail swishing.

The skulk was all there, with Haiki sitting quietly by Flint. He ran to me when he saw me. "Isla, I was so worried." As he licked my muzzle and settled beside me, relief fluttered along my tail. Between Siffrin and his Elders, and this unknown skulk, at least there was someone else like me— someone who didn't belong.

I gave Haiki a quick lick on the nose and turned to face Siffrin. My legs still wobbled but my voice was steady. "You've been searching for me?"

Siffrin spoke softly. "I looked to Canista's Lights. I was determined to find you."

My eyes darted to Haiki. He caught my gaze with an anxious frown. I turned back to Siffrin. The blood had been washed from his pelt and his scars were scarcely visible beneath his thick fur. Only a gash along his snout still glistened red.

"You seem well."

"It's because of you." His ears pointed sideways. "A young fox with no training shouldn't be any good at maa-sharm. But I knew I felt something that time on the roof—and today it was undeniable. Your maa is special . . . Still, you must be exhausted."

"I'm all right." I ran my tongue over my muzzle, my back stiffening. "I'm not sure why you came. You know that I'm seeking my brother. I don't have time for anything else."

Siffrin's eyes sparkled, amber framed in black. "The Mage will hunt you down when he learns of your gifts. He may know already . . . These lands are full of his spies. I want to lead you to safety—to the only place in the Wildlands where even the Mage cannot touch you. Let me take you to the Elder Rock."

10

"I'm not coming with you to the Elders." I stared back at Siffrin in challenge. "I told you: I'm going to find my brother."

Siffrin's ears flicked back. "They know more foxcraft than anyone else. They may have ways of finding him."

"That's what Haiki said." I wasn't convinced.

The gray-furred fox cleared his throat. "I've heard it's hard to find the Elder Rock when you're not sure what you're looking for. Wouldn't it be easier to go with someone who knows the way?" He tilted his head toward Siffrin but didn't meet his eye.

"Hard?" sniffed Siffrin, some of his old superior tone creeping back. "More like impossible."

The fur rose at my hackles.

Arrogant fox.

"That's assuming I want to go at all." I sought out Rupus among the skulk. He was sitting in the shadows. "The Elders are selfish. They hoard foxcraft for themselves. Isn't that right?"

I expected the old fox to agree but instead he hunched quietly, lost in thought.

"We are foxes of the meadow," said Karo. "We don't want to get in the middle of a battle between the Elders and the Seer. Survival is a daily struggle—it's hard enough just avoiding the furless." She rose to her paws, her tail low. "Bad things happen. We can't stop to think about them too long. Not when there's a skulk to feed." She shook out her fur. "I'm going hunting."

Flint sprang to his paws. "I'll come too."

"Do you hunt together?" I asked in surprise.

"Not in the way you mean," said Karo. "Not like wolves or dogs—we are not a pack. A fox is a lone hunter, but we share the kill. No one in this skulk goes hungry." She made for the tunnel.

Flint started after her. "Let's all get some air. It would do us good. When darkness falls the Wildlands are stalked by pleached foxes. At least we know that they'll leave us alone while the sun is high."

We padded out into a cool sun. I must have slept a day and night in that burrow within the den. A flock of birds flew high overhead, cutting patterns in the sky. I took in a deep breath, relieved to drink in the sharp, sweet air of the meadow.

The smallest fox of the skulk sidled up to me shyly.

"I'm Mox, by the way." He pawed the ground.

"I'm Isla."

"I know." He looked up, looked down at his paws. They were smudged with gray, like his muzzle. "They say you can do foxcraft."

"A bit."

His bent tail started wagging. "I wish I'd seen you save the coyote . . . I mean, the Elder's messenger in disguise. Simmi and Tao told me about it! I couldn't come with them . . ." His long ears rolled back. "I'd love to know foxcraft, but I'm not like the others. Greatfa says I'm special, but I know it's not a good thing really. I was born without enough maa. It means I need to rest a lot." He gave his tail a shake, as though to say it didn't matter. "It's always been that way . . . You must have strong maa. You remind me of Liro."

"The fox that disappeared?"

Mox pressed closer. "I think *they* caught him. It's like Ma said, he was a sharp fox, and he was quick—too quick for the furless. But he hasn't appeared among the pleached foxes, either."

I was about to reply when one of the old vixens—Dexa or Mips, I wasn't sure which—called Mox over to her. "Come out of the sunlight, you know it gives you headaches."

He blinked at me and shuffled to the shade.

Karo and Flint were prowling across the grass. I saw them touch noses and part ways at a hedgerow. Simmi and Tao capered about as Mox settled down beside Dexa and Mips. He must have been from the same litter, but he looked much younger. He might have been a cub. The bones stuck out on his narrow back and his limbs seemed frail. He rested his gray-smudged muzzle on his paws and watched his boisterous brother and sister chase each other's tails.

I felt a pang of pity for Mox, not strong enough for their games.

The two old vixens huddled close to him protectively. One licked his ears while the other picked a burr from his flank.

Siffrin stood at a distance from the skulk, gazing toward the wood. I turned away from him, my tail drifting low. Haiki jogged over to me. "Isla, can I speak with you?" His voice was hushed.

"You don't need to ask permission. Where were you when the coyotes arrived?" I hadn't meant to sound accusing. I glanced over my shoulder. Siffrin had lowered his gaze. He was watching me, his ears pricked up.

"I woke up and felt trapped, down in the den with all those strangers. The old fox scares me a bit . . ." He shifted uneasily from paw to paw. "Everyone was asleep, it was so quiet. I just wanted some air . . . I went to the stream to drink, to clear my head. But then I heard the coyotes and hid. I was just beyond the nettles—close enough to smell the pack. I was sure they'd find me and tear me limb from limb." He shuddered. "I didn't mean to worry you. I wasn't leaving or anything like that. I wouldn't leave without you!"

"You can do what you like," I said sharply. "We aren't bound together."

Haiki winced, his gray tail drooping. Immediately I was sorry. The fug hanging over from maa-sharm was making me edgy. My ears rolled forward and I gave him a lick on the nose.

Haiki brightened. "It's only . . ." He glanced in Siffrin's direction. "Only I thought you might reconsider. You know, about going to the Elders. I still think they're the best hope we have, and if the messenger is willing to take us—to take *you*, but maybe I could come—well, that's worth thinking about." His ears twisted. "I miss my skulk. Being with these foxes is such a relief, after so much time alone. But seeing them all together, so happy . . . It's hard. Do you know what I mean?"

My tail curved around my flank. I did know.

"If the Elders can help us, don't you think it's worth a try?" He glanced around, spotting Siffrin, who had started grooming his coat.

I flexed my whiskers. Was I being needlessly stubborn? *Could* the Elders help us?

Haiki threw another wary glance toward Siffrin. "Is it the Elders you're worried about? Or is it the messenger himself?"

I ran my claws along the dirt between two blades of grass. "I met Siffrin in the Snarl. I thought he was helping me, but he didn't tell me everything he knew. Important stuff, stuff that changes things. I'm worried that the Elders won't tell us much either."

"The messenger—Siffrin—he said they wanted you to come to the Elder Rock for your own protection. What makes you think they wouldn't help once you get there?"

Simmi and Tao were batting each other near the entrance to the den. They turned their heads in our direction.

"I don't understand it myself," I murmured as the two young foxes gamboled toward us. Their ears were back and they panted cheerfully. They had obviously decided to be friendly.

Simmi was breathless. "Do you want to see our patch?"

Tao's brush was wagging. "The territory has a stream right through the middle of it, and lots of places to hunt or sleep."

"It's probably the best patch in all the Upper Wildlands." Simmi's chest puffed up with pride.

"Please show us!" yelped Haiki with feeling.

"This way!" Tao cut a path between the nettles. Simmi hurried after him and Haiki followed. For a moment I paused, inclining my head so I could see Siffrin from the corner of my eye. He was still sitting in the same place but he was no longer looking my way.

We padded through grass and edged around bracken. Soon I could hear the gurgling of a stream.

When we found it, I stopped for a grateful drink. The water tingled the back of my throat, and I felt refreshed when I lifted my dripping muzzle.

I peered out over the meadow. I noticed a raised peak in the distance. "What's that hillock covered in heather? It looks like a good place for a view over the patch." Silently, I added, *And a good place to try gerra-sharm—to reach out to my brother.*

Simmi's eyes glittered. "We'll take you there!" She led the way with excited prances. We slid between leafy bracken, the earth gently swelling before us. The stream reappeared, weaving its route through the meadow. We trod alongside it for several brush-lengths before it dived away at a sharp angle and hurried off toward the woods. I remembered the coyote chief, alone on the white rock. Was his pack still in mourning? What would they do now that he'd gone?

A blood sun is risen!

I wondered what death meant to coyotes—what they believed.

My thoughts drifted to Farraclaw, the wolf from the beast dens. He had spoken of the hunt, with its honor and death.

A single beast, a single heart, as the hooves of your quarry beat a path like thunder. To risk the stampede; to sacrifice yourself, so that the Bishar survives. Never dead. Never forgotten. Always alive in the howls of the living.

Cubs of Canista, but so different from us.

I saw no honor in death. It was a dark void, a yearning emptiness. Sorrow crept along my fur and I pushed it away. There was no point howling at the moon or whimpering beneath the sun—it wouldn't bring my family back.

As we reached the heather-topped hillock, I could see where grass gave over to forest. Had the wolf made it through the Wildlands? Or had the furless caught up with him and wrestled him back into a cage?

"Up here," Simmi panted, scaling the top of the hillock.

The landscape opened up before us. Padding in a circle, I took in hawthorn bushes and lush green pastures. A couple of rabbits were out on the meadow. I caught a flash of ginger fur: Karo was stalking toward them. Her shoulders glided above the long grass. She paused, watching the rabbits as they hopped a few paces and started to nibble at shrubs.

"Our territory goes up to the woods in the North, and the hazels in the East," said Simmi proudly. "Ma and Fa are the best hunters. Dexa and Mips mostly catch small prey like mice and voles. They tend to stay near the den."

"We're getting pretty good at hunting too!" declared Tao.

"I wish we knew some foxcraft," Simmi whined. "We'd

be the terror of rabbits everywhere! Pleached foxes wouldn't dare creep around the meadow at night." She glanced thoughtfully over her patch. "They never used to be so brave."

Tao's tail was thrashing wildly. "You heard what Greatfa said. We don't need the Elders and their foxcraft! I trapped a squirrel last week all on my own."

"It had a broken leg," Simmi pointed out.

Tao growled at her. "So what? It was still hard to catch! And everyone got to try a bit."

I was impressed by how this large skulk worked together for their survival. "How about Mox?" I asked, still looking out over the meadow. From the corner of my eye, I saw Simmi and Tao exchange a look.

"He tried some too," said Tao. "A leg, I think."

"That's not what Isla meant." Simmi crept closer to me. "Mox doesn't hunt," she said in a hushed voice, though we were nowhere near the other foxes. "We don't expect him to . . . He eats from the skulk's cache."

"It isn't his fault," Tao put in quickly. "He was sick when he was born, and he never really recovered."

I was touched by their loyalty. I couldn't imagine an ailing newborn surviving long in the Great Snarl.

Tao shook his fur. "It must be completely different where you come from, Isla."

I thought of the endless graystone and the dark, jagged walls. "The furless are everywhere in huge numbers. And their dens—you can hardly move for their dens."

"They build aboveground, don't they?" asked Haiki. "Not like us."

"Not like rabbits!" added Tao. "There are furless in the Wildlands, though they're more scattered here. They're dangerous, though. Particularly hunters."

Alarm crossed Haiki's face. "A hunter chased us."

Simmi cocked her head. "You were lucky to escape. That's why we rarely leave the patch. Most of the furless live toward the Graylands. Not that you can really avoid them. They're everywhere. Can you see that dark strip at the edge of the forest?"

We looked out over the bushes.

"That's the deathway. The furless stalk along it in manglers."

I caught sight of the graystone. I hadn't realized that the deathway traveled this far. "There's nowhere beyond their reach," I murmured. "The furless have carved up the world and made it theirs."

Tao flashed a conspiratorial look. "There is one place. Up in the Snowlands, beyond the Raging River. It's so cold there that even the furless stay away."

Simmi's eyes sparkled with savage delight. "But you

wouldn't want to end up there." She lowered her voice. "They say that the wind is so sharp it whips the fur from your skin, and the snow is so cold that it freezes the blood. Malinta scarcely reaches the Snowlands. But that's not even the worst of it! Snow wolves prowl the tundra in packs—giant beasts who'll tear you to shreds!" She spun with a shriek and leaped on Tao, who rolled in surprise. He chased her down the hillock through the heather. Haiki barked excitedly, racing after them. I watched as the three young foxes bounded over the grassy meadow. My tail twitched with excitement but I held back.

I used to play like that with Pirie.

Alone on the hillock, I called to him. "Where are you?"

The wind whistled through the heather. The stream gurgled over the rocks. High overhead, a lone crow cawed.

But my brother did not answer.

11

"Pirie? Pirie, are you there?"

"I'm just behind you."

I craned my neck. He was standing on the frosty grass at the edge of the frozen circle. He tapped a forepaw on the ice but held back. "Can you feel the heat of the sun yet?"

The pigeon gray of the sky was tinged with white streaks. My fur felt damp along my back, even though no rain fell. The fence to our patch was licked with frost.

My paw pads ached with cold. I took another step over the ice. "The sun must be trapped very deep. I can't feel any heat at all." I lowered my muzzle and sniffed. Did the sun have a scent? The ice didn't smell of anything. Squinting, I took in its silvery shimmer, and the touches of gold that glanced across the surface—the sun was down there, but how would we reach it?

I took another step, my forepaw skidding, and yelped in frustration. It was like learning to walk for the first time.

Pirie snorted.

"It's harder than it looks!"

He cocked his head. "I believe you."

We'd agreed that only one of us should cross the frozen circle. The other would watch out for Greatma, Ma, or Fa. They'd be grateful, of course, once we'd rescued the sun, but if they caught us in the act we knew they wouldn't understand.

I was the one to find the sun. It was up to me to investigate. I'd insisted that Pirie stay on the grass—but that was before I knew how hard it was to walk on ice.

I turned back to the frozen circle. I wanted to reach the middle—that's where the golden light was brightest—that's where I'd feel the sun's warmth. I wasn't sure what I'd do when I got there. Maybe dig a hole so that it could escape. How big was the sun? Beyond the clouds, it never seemed large, but it was hard to tell.

I felt a cool fizzle on my ear and looked up. The white streaks of the sky had grown longer, looping against the gray. A small wisp swirled down to rest on my nose. As I lapped at it, it melted on my tongue. Another flake landed before me on the ice.

"It's snowing!" yelped Pirie. I tried to turn but my paws slipped beneath me. I spun along the frozen circle and flopped onto my belly. Pirie snorted in amusement. As if he'd do any better! I snarled at him but excitement tingled at my fur-tips. I scrambled onto my forepaws and sent myself whirling, this time on purpose, my tail flying up in the air. The snow was falling more heavily. Yet each flake was so delicate and light it was a wonder they didn't just float in the sky like tiny winged insects. I snapped at the falling snow, enjoying the icy fizz on my tongue.

When I slid to a stop I'd come much further into the frozen circle. I blinked the wisps from my lashes and looked around. Snow fell thickly in the neighboring patch. Already the trees were growing white and a twinkling pelt coated the fence. The world of the furless—the land of graystone and brittle walls—was fading into softness. Snowflakes landed with a whisper, disguising the sound of pawsteps over frost.

I yelped in alarm. Between cool twists of white I saw a pair of amber eyes.

Pirie shrilled back. "What is it?"

I drew in my breath, my legs rigid against the ice. It wasn't any warmer here after all. A shiver ran along my back. A large male fox was watching me. Snow clung to his fur as his long brush drifted back and forth. The white tip quivered in question or threat—I couldn't be sure.

Pirie must have spotted him. "Stay away from her!" he spat. To me, he spoke in an urgent breath. "Come over here, Isla. We need to get back to the den."

My heart started thumping. Strangers were dangerous—Greatma had told us that dozens of times. I started scrambling over the ice. I was moving much more quickly now, but my legs refused to obey my commands. They thrashed and slipped beneath me, struggling to keep me upright. I smacked against the circle with a clunk. Something cracked under my belly. I panicked, afraid I had hurt myself, but as I lay still the pain didn't come.

The bite of icy water.

I shrank back, alarmed. The ice had splintered across the circle as though sliced by a talon. As it parted, I saw no hint of the sun. Water splashed over the growing gap, freezing and depthless.

"The ice is breaking!" I squinted through the heavy snowfall, seeking Pirie, but I'd lost my bearings. Instead of my brother, I saw the large fox. He was rising, his black legs stark against the whitening yard.

He stalked toward the cracking circle, his cool eyes fixed on me.

The sky was growing dark as Karo and Flint returned to the den. Karo carried two large rabbits in her jaws. Flint dropped a third in a heap alongside them. Dexa, Mips, and Siffrin had gathered a bird and several mice.

Simmi, Tao, and Mox yipped like cubs. They panted

and thrashed their tails, rushing at their parents, just as Pirie and I had greeted ours after a hunt.

"We cached another rabbit," said Flint, giving me and Haiki a gently mocking look. "This can be eaten straight-away. That is, if everyone's hungry."

Haiki watched, his ears twisting forward and back.

"We're *starving*!" yelped Mox.

Tao was drumming his forepaws on the ground.

Simmi was the first to bite down on a rabbit. The rest of the skulk fell upon the kill, tearing and gnashing. My belly rumbled but I held back warily. It wasn't my skulk. I'd already stolen their food—I didn't need Flint to remind me of that.

Apparently Haiki didn't share my concerns. He scooped a mouse into his jaws and snarfed it greedily. Even Siffrin was eating, crunching on the bird at the edge of the nettles. He gulped down a mouthful and met my eye. His gaze was challenging. *What are you waiting for?* it seemed to say. Did he mean the kill, or something else?

I edged forward. Tao was wrestling one of the rabbits. I seized on a dangling back leg and we tussled it between us before falling back with our own hunks of meat.

Bellies full, we climbed into the den. I settled along the wall, licking my paws. I thought of the skulk's easy generos-ity. I remembered how friendly Haiki had been when I'd first met him. Both were far from the hostility I'd encoun-tered in the Great Snarl, even from my own kind. I pictured the elderly vixen who'd chased me out of a wildway on my first night alone. Then I remembered what had happened to her. The snatchers had grabbed her roughly and carried her away, beyond a yellow door where foxes were taken and never came back.

Graylands foxes had reason to be wary.

The skulk stretched out across the den, washing them-selves. An air of calm fell over the foxes. Even Simmi and Tao were relaxed, grooming Mox's fur. Haiki padded to my side and shuffled onto his belly with a yawn. "Rabbit is so tasty."

"It is," I agreed, lapping my muzzle. I looked up to see Siffrin watching. He held my gaze, then turned and started along the tunnel.

I rose to my paws.

Haiki stared at me. "Where are you going? We only just came inside."

"I need to talk to Siffrin."

"I'll come with you." He started to rise.

"I'll be back soon." I had to do this alone.

His ears flattened. "Are you sure?" Flint turned his dark head in our direction and Haiki spoke more quietly. "There's something not quite right about Siffrin . . . Like he knows more than he's saying." He pawed me anxiously. "I wish you'd stay here, with me and the skulk. What if he tries to harm you with foxcraft?"

I was touched by Haiki's concern. "I'm not scared of Siffrin." I gave the gray-furred fox a quick lick on the nose and stepped away before he could say any more. I ignored the curious glances of the skulk as I wove between them and into the tunnel.

Siffrin was standing among the nettles, just where he'd appeared in the guise of a coyote. His thick brush swept the grass in a rhythmic movement. Behind him the moon rose in the sky.

"I didn't know if you'd come," he said.

"I thought I'd hear what you had to say."

He tilted his head. "The valley is quiet. The Taken are most active when the moon sets. Let's go by the stream where we won't be overheard."

My ears twisted. Who did he think might be listening? Was he worried about the skulk? Siffrin's words awakened a new fear—what if Karo and Flint had their own reasons for letting us stay?

Siffrin's tail swished as he turned and stalked through the nettles. My ears flicked back. He assumed I would follow him.

I padded at a distance.

He led us over the gentle incline of the meadow along the winding path of the stream. He paused at a hazel bush, his snout punching the air, before he settled down on a bed of moss.

I sat opposite, watching warily. There were so many questions I'd wanted to ask him, so many things I needed to say. But now, in the darkness of the meadow, I forgot what they were.

Siffrin was the first to speak. "When the snatchers took you away, I thought that was the end of you." His right ear twitched. "I had no choice but to return to the Wildlands. I went straight to Jana, to tell her what had happened. I was surprised when she said you were still alive."

"How did she know?"

"An Elder called Mika told her. Mika has a way of sensing these things."

"Foxcraft?"

He caught my eye. "A state called 'pashanda.' Only the Elders can do it, and Mika's their expert. They enter into a kind of trance and summon knowledge from the wind."

"And Pirie? Did she sense him too?"

"I don't know." Siffrin glanced down at a forepaw. "I only saw Jana. I told her what I'd seen in maa-sharm after the Taken skulk caught up with us. She agreed that you're special. She thought it would be dangerous for you to wander alone."

My tail flicked irritably. "I've managed this far."

"The journey to the Elder Rock is hazardous. There is

the deathway, woodlands, and a path that appears with the last brush of dusk. Old forces defend the lands surrounding the Rock. Not all who search will find what they are looking for. And you'll be followed too, you won't get far. The Mage will know about you from Karka."

"Karka's dead," I said flatly.

Siffrin looked up in surprise. "You didn't . . . ?"

"Not me." I thought of the wolf from the beast dens. He'd killed the Mage's assassin as though it was nothing. I remembered the fierce, brutal power of the wolf's mighty jaws and the blood that clung to his maw.

"But the Taken knew," said Siffrin. "They knew about you. And that means that the Mage must know about you too."

I glowered. "And I suppose they know what he did to my family."

Siffrin winced. "I should have told you the truth right away, but please understand. I had instructions to find Pirie. I thought that if you knew what had happened you wouldn't let me help you. We are in the midst of a war for the freedom of our kind—I had to put the Elders first. I didn't know you then. Once I did, it was too late to tell you."

My fur itched. "Oh, I understand. I understand that you used me." My eyes trailed down to his foreleg, dark in the moonlight. "All this talk of Jana and the Elders. But I've seen your secret—it's scorched on your flesh."

Siffrin's tail twitched. "You know I'm not one of the Taken. You can't possibly think—"

"Then why do you carry the mark?"

"If you hate me so much, why did you give me maa-sharm?"

We glared at each other. In the silence that followed, the stream seemed to grow louder, hissing as the water leaped over pebbles. Siffrin raised his muzzle to the moon. "I was a much younger cub than you are now. I lived in the Marshlands—I told you that, didn't I? I remember the tufty grasses and watery ponds with large yellow flowers, and the clouds of mosquitoes that closed in at dusk. It's my family I've forgotten. Perhaps I was part of a large litter. I have a sense that there were other cubs around me—a feeling of ease, the hint of a soothing smell. Even my ma's face has vanished from my memories. Whether she was lean, tall, good at hunting. The color of her coat."

I frowned, watching Siffrin. "Did the Taken come after you? Did they give you that mark on your foreleg?"

"The Taken can't perform foxcraft—they can't steal another fox's will. It takes the Narral to do that."

"The Mage's inner guard?"

Siffrin dipped his head. "Like Karka . . . The Narral are experts in foxcraft. If you see a skulk of Taken, and one is a free fox, run for your life!"

I shuddered, remembering the one-eyed vixen.

"In my case, the Mage didn't send an assassin," said Siffrin. "Back then, there probably wasn't anyone else. He hadn't yet found the source of his power, but he must have been seeking it with the full cunning of his ambition. I can't say if he had a brush—I've heard that it's missing, but I honestly don't remember."

"The Tailless Seer," I mumbled.

Siffrin's ears flicked back. "That's what they call him here. The one that turns fertile lands to ruin."

"What happened to your family?" I asked, though I already knew.

"He killed them. My ma and fa, the rest of the skulk. The other cubs too. I don't know why he spared me." Siffrin's voice was cool. "Jana thinks that it could have been an early test, to see if he could extract my will."

"Sorry . . . About your family."

Siffrin glanced at me, his eyes blank. "It was a long time ago."

I watched him uncertainly. "The foxes here say that the Mage's skulk are 'pleached.'" I remembered Flint's words. *We call them "pleached" because of what's been done to them.* "So pleaching . . . It can be reversed?"

"Not easily. The thing that's stolen must be released," he said vaguely.

"The will?"

"No, I mean . . ." He trailed off. "Run fast, be safe, live free," he added in a whisper.

"There are so many pleached foxes. Where do they all come from—the Taken? Haiki calls them that too."

"He isn't from around here?"

"He's from the lowlands."

"Not far from the marshes, where I come from." Siffrin inclined his head slightly.

"So I was right, the Mage left that scar on your foreleg?"

The red-furred fox flexed his paw. "I was very young—I couldn't have put up much of a fight." He closed his eyes. "I tried to get away from him. He snapped at me and yanked me back. I remember a stab of pain."

"He bit your foreleg."

Siffrin opened his eyes. "Why do you say that?"

"That's where you carry the mark. That's where *all* the Taken bear a wound."

Siffrin looked down at his foreleg, as though he'd forgotten the rose-shaped scar. "That makes sense. It was so long ago . . ." He gave himself a shake. "Jana found me alone in the Wildlands. She undid the Mage's curse. She saved me from a fate worse than death and raised me as her own."

His words had awakened a memory inside me. I looked beyond the moon and caught the faintest glimmer of

Canista's Lights. I recalled a cub beneath shadowy trees, and pictured an old gray fox.

Siffrin's eyes were blazing. "Now do you understand? Now can you see why I'm so grateful to her—why she and the Elders mean so much to me? They're the only family I've ever known, the only ones I can remember. And they're all that protects us from the Mage."

I could feel my anger waning. Picturing him as a small, scared cub, I did understand. "Why can't they just kill him?"

Siffrin batted away a stem of grass. "It isn't that simple. Foxcraft can sap a fox's maa, you know that yourself now. It would take extraordinary strength to pleach a whole army—if pleaching really is how the Mage controls his victims. He must be gaining the power somewhere. He is stronger than he *should* be. Even the Elders are at a loss."

"Is pleaching a foxcraft?" I'd asked Flint the same question but he hadn't replied. Perhaps he didn't know.

Siffrin glanced over his shoulder. He sniffed the air, his whiskers bristling. When he turned back to me, his voice was so low that I strained to hear him over the stream. "A rare and dangerous one," he breathed. "Its practice is a closely guarded secret that the Elders have sworn to take to their deaths, as have all Elders before them." He cast a look into the darkness. "Only among the Elders themselves should pleaching be performed. I cannot guess how it is done and Jana would never tell me—it is against foxlore to speak of pleaching beyond the Rock. If the Mage has learned its ways we are in greater peril than I'd ever imagined."

I took in the sounds of the night, the hoots and chirps, the rustling of leaves. The heather-topped hillock was a gray silhouette. I had stood there, calling to Pirie, and been met with silence. Where would I go?

I thought of the Elders with their special powers. One of them—Mika?—had sensed me. What if she could help me find Pirie? My brow crinkled. "If the Elders are the only foxes who know how to pleach, how come the Mage can do it?"

Siffrin swallowed, his tail flicking against the grass. "Two of the Elders have disappeared."

His meaning dawned on me. "When we met in the Snarl, you said the Black Fox was missing. You think—"

My words were cut short by a distant volley of gekkers.

"The Taken," hissed Siffrin. He darted along the grassy bank toward the den. For a moment I stood still, bewildered by what he'd told me. The Mage was amassing an army of blank-eyed foxes, drawing upon some unknown power. He knew foxcraft that was never performed beyond the Rock.

That could mean only one thing.

The Mage was an Elder.

12

Night stole slowly into my dreams, muddled with shards of memory. I pictured my old patch, but not as I'd known it. The grass was dappled with warming light. A blizzard of tiny white flowers hung over the fence and tall blue posies bobbed their heads on the breeze. Butterflies danced loops in the sky. I pounced at them, but they slipped through my outstretched paws like air. I gamboled through the flowers in search of my family. The den was empty. A small patch of mottled fur clung to the entrance—Pirie's fur, or Greatma's. I took a sniff but it smelled of nothing.

I padded to the wildway on the far side of the fence. As I climbed over the broken branch, a pelt of cloud drew over the sky. In a pawstep, the world changed. Frost shimmered at the base of the branch, leading to a frozen midnight world. It wasn't the wildway that I had known—a grassy yard walled in by fences. There were no borders to the land. It stretched in all directions, sparkling with frost, fading to darkness. My paws crunched on the frozen ground as I padded beneath the trees.

"Greatma? Pirie?"

My voice came back to me as an echo. My ears rotated and I paused, forepaw suspended. Two ravens wheeled overhead.

Flesh-eating birds. That's what Fa had called them. "Scavengers, they feast on rotting meat."

Back in the Wildlands, when he was a cub, his skulk had trailed ravens across pastures—it was an easy way to find a meal during times of hunger.

"Don't be scared, they're helpful," he'd assured me and Pirie. "Follow the ravens and you'll find the kill." I looked to the twisting pelt of the sky. The ravens were barely visible, slick feathers against dark clouds. I started padding between the trees, weaving a path through the frost. In time, the ground grew mulchy beneath my paws. More trees appeared, expanding in all directions. Their branches bent and grasped like talons.

Whiskers tensed, I crept deeper into the forest. The cry of the ravens made my fur stand on end.

Flesh-eating birds. The fur rose along my back.

Follow the ravens and you'll find the kill.

The forest around me grew denser and deeper. I shrank

back, hurrying toward the fence. But as I retraced my steps, the trees hunched together, blocking my way. Their long branches wove in angled knots. Was I heading in the right direction? A peculiar smell caught my nose—the whiff of something sour. Yellow mushrooms peeked up from the mulchy earth. My eyes stung with their rancid smell.

I turned again, confused. The trees were all around me. The mushrooms seemed to be shuffling closer. I ran away from the stench of decay, but the forest wove ahead of me. A screech above and my head shot up. The ravens were wheeling in circles, drifting lower. Their dark eyes glittered in the failing light.

They weren't leading me anywhere.

I was leading them.

"Isla, wake up." Haiki was gazing down on me. His soft brown eyes and fluffy face drew me out of my dark dreams. "It's dawn," he said. "Rupus has an idea."

I shook my fur. The skulk was awakening, stretching and yawning. Straining to hear, I caught no sound of the ghoulish Taken over the Ghost Valley. They must have retreated with the first light.

The old fox was sitting by the entrance to the tunnel, his forepaws folded under him. Further along the wall, Siffrin was grooming his coat.

I rubbed my eyes with a forepaw. "What sort of idea?"

I'd spoken softly, but Rupus heard me. "I saw your friend returning from a late drink at the stream. I asked him if he still planned to find the Elders."

I watched Siffrin from the corner of my eye. He stiffened, studying Rupus with interest. Flint and Karo exchanged glances and Simmi nudged Tao.

"I said . . ." Haiki swallowed, uneasy before the gaze of the skulk. "I thought it was the only way. The only way to find my family."

"But it isn't just about your family, is it, gray fox?" Rupus's small eyes were searching. "Nor Isla's brother, or any one of us. It is, after all, about *all* of us."

I glanced at Siffrin. Hadn't he said something similar back in the Great Snarl?

Rupus spoke with grim determination. "I have never had much patience for the Elders, but we are under attack. It is said that the Darklands have doubled in size since the last gloaming. The Deep Forest has expanded into the Marshlands. At the borders of the Darklands, meadows perish."

I shivered at the memory of my dream.

Rupus shook his head. "When my ma and fa settled here many malintas back, it was to escape the furless, whose range had grown far beyond the limits of the Graylands. Where they came, the deathway appeared, and where the deathway led, more furless followed. We always believed them to be the greatest menace. But a new threat has risen, even deadlier than the furless, because it knows what we are and it knows how to find us. In time, our meadow will also rot."

"It won't!" yelped Flint. "We'll defend it."

Simmi and Tao barked in agreement, slamming their forepaws on the ground.

Karo sprang up, her long tail swishing. "We'd rather die than let it fall to the Seer."

"And die you shall, if nothing is done." Rupus ran his cool gaze over the skulk, pausing at Siffrin and ending with me and Haiki. "Or worse, you'll become one of them. One of the 'Taken,' as these young foxes call them. It is only a matter of time."

Karo screwed up her pointy snout. "Canista's Lights shine bright on the longest day of the year. The earth will be full of maa. With the power of the gloaming, we'll defend ourselves."

"The gloaming," snorted Rupus. His voice rose in anger. "Don't you see, we won't make it to the gloaming! The way things are going, we will scarcely survive malinta."

Karo dropped her head. Perhaps she sensed her fa was right.

One of the old vixens spoke. "What of the Free Lands to the east?"

Mox buried his head against her belly. "They're so far," he whimpered. "There are hills, and lakes, and furless dens. Wild animals live in the ranges beneath the Raging River, and I've heard there's scarcely any food . . ." The little fox must have known he wouldn't have the strength for such a journey.

"We're not going to the Free Lands." Rupus shook his skinny tail. "If we start running now, we'll be running forever. If we hope to survive, we'll need more than our courage and a deep-buried den." He turned to Siffrin with a hard look. "I want you to take us to the Elders. We must learn the secrets of foxcraft."

Siffrin's muzzle was firm, his amber eyes thoughtful. "I cannot take a whole skulk. Isla could come with me. We could seek the Elders' counsel on your behalf."

I was about to protest. Quietly, I'd decided to go to the Elders, but I hadn't shared this thought with Siffrin.

"Not good enough," snapped Rupus before I could speak. "With the greatest respect, Isla's not of our skulk—and neither are you."

Siffrin's brush was twitching. "So many foxes moving through the Wildlands . . . someone would see us."

"Not all of us, then. A couple of our quickest young foxes." Rupus looked over the skulk. "Take Simmi and Tao."

They yipped and barked enthusiastically. Mox gave a small whine and slouched against the wall, gathering his tail around him.

Siffrin was quiet a long time. When he spoke at last he was resolute. "I would like to help you, but we'd never make it across the shana."

I ran my tongue over my muzzle. "What do you mean, the 'shana'?" I had heard the term before.

He turned his amber eyes on me. "It's a ring of maa that the Elders weave around the Rock in a secret ritual called 'shana-sharm.' Without it, the Mage might attack any time. Even the Elders couldn't fend off an army of Taken." Siffrin turned back to Rupus. "Given everything that's happening, the Elders will be wary. They won't let strangers pass. Jana knows about Isla, but she can't know of your skulk. I need to go ahead to assure her that it's safe. I can return for Isla, Simmi, and Tao if she agrees. It's the best I can do."

Simmi's shoulders sank with disappointment. "If you let him go without us, he'll never come back."

"I will. I promise." Siffrin met her gaze and Simmi blinked at him curiously. My ears flipped back. How dare the red-furred fox make decisions without checking with me! I hadn't said that I'd go to the Elders. But Haiki's brown eyes willed me to agree.

"When will you return?" I asked.

"If I run all the way, stopping only to rest, I can be back by the third moon. Then I'll lead you to the Elders with Simmi and Tao."

A muffled whimper escaped Haiki's throat. I thought of him left behind with the skulk, never knowing what became of his family. Going to the Elders was his idea—it was practically the first thing he'd said when we'd met.

"And Haiki," I added.

Siffrin's tail-tip fluttered. "And Haiki."

The sun was climbing over the meadow as Siffrin padded through the tunnel and out toward the nettles. Haiki and the Wildlands skulk held back at the entrance of the den.

I rushed forward. "Don't go yet."

Siffrin turned back to me in surprise. "What is it? You will come with me, won't you? When I return?"

"I'll come with you to the Elders."

The tension left his face and he sighed with relief.

But I hadn't finished. "Before you go . . ." I glanced back at the skulk, then took a few paces toward him so I was out of earshot. "Teach me wa'akkir."

Siffrin stiffened. "Isla, I can't . . ."

I pushed ahead of him, stalking through the nettles. "Of course you can."

He padded behind me. "It's a complex foxcraft. Foxlore insists it is only for those trained in the higher arts. A fox must study his subject, mimicking their movements and behavior. There are important rules that accompany its practice."

I frowned impatiently. "What sort of rules?"

"Like not all creatures should be mimicked—wa'akkir is only for cubs of Canista. You could shift into a dog or a coyote, but not into, I don't know . . . a squirrel. They're too different from us. It would be dangerous, unstable."

"I wouldn't!"

"Misuse is—"

"I know. As long as I don't meet the creature I've mimicked, I'm sure I'll be fine," I added slyly.

"There's more to it than that."

"But it can't cause anyone harm—not like pleaching."

Siffrin sighed. "It can cause *you* harm."

I wound through the grass to the bank of the stream. "It's tiring, I get it. I'll only shape-shift if I really have to."

Siffrin paused by the side of the stream. "Wa'akkir is a higher art. It drains maa. Staying too long in the altered state leads to premature aging. Everything withers, like a fallen leaf."

Despite myself, my ears flipped back. "I'll be careful. I won't just turn into anyone."

Siffrin looked stern. "It isn't that you'd actually change. It's an illusion, like slimmering. You'd still smell like yourself. Others might sense an impostor, especially those trained in foxcraft themselves. Your true nature cannot always be concealed."

I remembered the first time I'd met Siffrin, in the shape of a wiry dog. A dog with no shadow, whose reflection against shimmering spy holes revealed a red-furred fox. But there were no spy holes in the Wildlands, away from furless dens, and shadows were lost among thickets of leaves.

Siffrin licked his paw pad. "I'm leaving, Isla. Why don't you come with me? The Elders may instruct you in wa'akkir. They're better teachers than I am."

I glanced back toward the nettles. "Leave without the others?"

"It would be safer."

My lip twitched over my fangs. I couldn't believe what I was hearing. "I'm not just going to abandon foxes who've helped me. And I need to know how to perform wa'akkir. Could you tell me the chant? I can work out the rest."

Siffrin stamped the ground with his forepaw. "Isla, it isn't just about the chant. You're not old enough and frankly I doubt you're wise enough for the higher arts."

Anger crackled along my fur. "I knew it wouldn't be long until you spoke down to me." I glared at him, a snarl in my throat. "You think you're so clever, hoarding wa'akkir to yourself!"

"For the final time . . ." He didn't finish. His amber eyes grew round.

"What is it?" I hissed.

"Get down!"

It was then that I saw one of the scrawny dogs from the gorge. I dropped onto my belly. My eyes scanned the long grass of the meadow. "Be careful," I whispered. "There's another one."

Siffrin frowned, his nostrils pulsing. "Only one?"

The soil trembled and the thump of paws disturbed the grass. Two stout dogs hurried out from behind a tree, a gingery one with floppy ears and a dirty white dog with a shaggy coat. The black-and-tan from the gorge trotted after them.

Taking the lead was the tall dog that Haiki had tricked. This time, he had his whole pack around him. My belly flipped as more dogs shuffled out from under a briar bush.

Their lips curled back over pointed jaws, their muscles tensed for a fight.

13

Flattening my body, I did my best to melt into the grass. It was harder for Siffrin. He was much larger than me, with a thick red brush that refused to be concealed.

"They'll see you," I mouthed. I could tell they had already smelled us from their rigid bodies. The larger dog from the gorge swiveled his head. His muzzle was pulsing, a snarl in his throat. Haiki's trick meant I'd escaped him before. If he saw me again, he would take his revenge.

Siffrin's lips were uttering the faintest words.

"I am the fur that ruffles your back. I am the twist and shake of your tail. Let me appear in the shape of your body: no one can tell; others will fear; dare not come near!"

From the corner of my eye, I saw the dogs pause to sniff the earth. What was Siffrin doing?

The air around him grew soft, a cloud of red fur. The

black-and-tan dog had paused and was looking in our direction. Her ears pricked up and she growled.

I thrummed with panic.

They're going to see him!

Was it worth a quick yip of alarm? I opened my mouth. But before I could make a sound, Siffrin disappeared from view. My jaw hung open. I sniffed the air, my whiskers springing forward. I could smell the sweet, rich tang of his coat. I realized he was still there, pressed upon the grass. Instead of twisting his shape into a terrible beast, he'd turned into a tiny, sandy-furred creature—the smallest dog I had ever seen.

The black-and-tan cocked her head in confusion. She barked to the others, who shot around to look at her.

"What is it?" snapped the tall, dark-furred dog. "A rabbit?"

"Something moved in the grass! At first it looked like . . . like a fox with a big red tail. But a moment later I saw a small dog. Then it disappeared."

"Well, which one was it? A rabbit, a fox or . . . What was the other one?" There was a snide edge to the tall dog's voice.

"Disappeared?" yelped the white dog with the shaggy fur. "Have you been chewing canarygrass again?"

The other dogs snorted and yapped, despite having been on guard themselves only a moment ago.

Siffrin's eyes were sharp when they found mine. "Slimmer," he mouthed. "Now!"

I recited the chant without making a sound.

What was seen is unseen; what was sensed becomes senseless. What was bone is bending; what was fur is air.

Siffrin shuffled forward on his belly, wending a slow path through the grass. He was slimmering while in wa'ak-kir, layering one foxcraft on top of another with practiced expertise. The tiny frame of the sandy-furred dog barely grazed the grass stems as he slid between them. Compared to him, I felt large and clumsy.

Slimmering came easier than it used to in the Snarl. With the chant, my eyes grew misty and my heartbeat slowed. My body relaxed to a steady rhythm. Stealthily I crept along the grass, my tail trailing behind me.

"There!" woofed the black-and-tan dog. "Did you see that? The grass moved!"

"The grass moved!" mimicked the pack leader to the yips and snarls of the other dogs. "The wind blew the grass! It must be a monster."

The black-and-tan scowled. "I can *smell* foxes. You must be able to smell them too?"

The shaggy white dog raised her muzzle. "There are foxes all over meadows like this. They usually sleep in the day, don't they? That scent trail must be old. They set it down for other foxes. *Everyone* knows that!"

"But it's familiar . . . I think it's the foxes from the bracken field. The gray and the cub who lied about the rabbits."

"That was *your* fault," snapped the pack leader, though it was he who had fallen for Haiki's trick, not the more suspicious black-and-tan. He turned to the others. "You can't trust foxes, that's what I told him, but would he listen?"

Rage rose off the black-and-tan's fur. If she caught us now she would make us suffer. I tried not to think about it as I followed a steady path toward Siffrin. He was making for a burst of hazel. Once we reached it, we would be out of the circle of hostile dogs. I held back my breath, though it pulsed in my throat. Not far now.

"Are you sure it wasn't Red you saw?" snarled the leader.

A stout, ginger dog responded with a bark, capering about with his stubby tail held high. "Look at me, I'm a fox! I've got a great big tail like a fluffy cat!"

The dogs barked raucously, mocking the black-and-tan. I tensed as they cut between me and Siffrin, unwittingly barring my escape.

The urge to breathe was squeezing at my throat. If I drew in breath, I'd be visible to them.

What was seen is unseen; what was sensed becomes senseless.

I was only faintly aware that Siffrin had reached the hazel bush and had broken from his slimmer. The figure of a tiny dog was well concealed beneath the spiky branches.

The pack leader yawned noisily. He had tired of his game. "I'm hungry. There's nothing to eat around here."

The others stopped playing, alert all at once.

"I saw rabbits on the other side of the meadow," said the scruffy white dog.

At last I sensed them move away. My chest quivered urgently, my throat felt thick. *Just a little longer,* I coaxed myself. *They've almost gone.*

What was bone is bending; what was fur is air.

One after another, the dogs padded after their leader, making for the valley downstream.

All except for the black-and-tan.

Stubbornly she hung back. She circled the tall grass, her muzzle trembling. If I tried to run, she would catch me. She trod so close that she almost stepped on my tail. I froze, too scared to move. My breath was screaming at my ribs. My head grew dizzy and my shoulders quivered.

My vision sharpened, the haze of the slimmer breaking away. I spotted my forepaws nestled in the grass.

The pelt of invisibility was lifting.

"You! How dare you enter my territory!"

I jerked up my head, the breath exploding from my mouth. I cringed against the earth, gasping for air, sure to feel the dog's teeth snap around my throat. The black-and-tan was only a brush-length before me but she didn't spare me a glance. Her gaze was fixed on the hazel bush.

Still panting, I raised my head.

The tiny dog was nowhere to be seen. Standing by the

hazel bush was a beast so savage that I cringed and scrambled backward. Her massive shoulders flexed with power, the muscles bunching beneath her slick black fur. Her limbs trembled with rage and her lips peeled back to reveal glistening fangs.

I had seen this dog before—back in the Snarl she'd guarded a furless yard. Except, of course, this wasn't a dog: Siffrin had shifted his shape again.

The black-and tan froze, her hackles up.

"I asked you a question," Siffrin growled.

Down on my belly, I scrambled through the grass, making for the ivy upstream. When I reached the cover of ferns, I looked around. The other dogs were stalking back, converging on the grass where I had slimmered. Had they gotten there a moment earlier . . .

The pack leader strode to the black-and-tan's side. "Who are you?" he barked. He tried to stand tall but his back legs trembled. Even surrounded by his pack, his fear of a confrontation was obvious.

"Why don't you come closer and find out?" growled Siffrin in wa'akkir.

Nobody moved.

Suddenly the great dog turned and bolted over the grass. "By the third moon!" she barked as she neared the bank of the stream. As she reached a copse, she vanished from view.

The bewildered pack exploded in a frenzy of yaps. They pounded over the grass, racing back and forth along the stream. They couldn't understand where the black dog had come from—or where she'd gone.

But I knew.

Concealed behind the safety of the ferns, I blinked rapidly. I saw through Siffrin's slimmer as he eased himself across the lake and climbed out onto the far bank. I watched as he wound between ferns to cut across the meadow while the unsuspecting dogs paced the near bank of the stream.

They snarled and yapped, glaring over the ferns. They didn't think to look beyond the water, at the hill dotted with straight-backed pines. They didn't notice the bright red fox as he gazed back over the grass, or see him turn to bound into the forest.

I sat amid the ferns long after the dogs had gone, repeating the wa'akkir chant. Sometimes I mumbled the words. Sometimes I uttered them in my mind.

I am the fur that ruffles your back. I am the twist and shake of your tail. Let me appear in the shape of your body: no one can tell; others will fear; dare not come near!

It made no difference. When I looked at my forepaws, they remained silky black. My tail was ginger, the tip still white.

It was more than the chant. There was a trick to wa'ak-kir, a special knack. There had to be. Why wouldn't Siffrin teach me? My whiskers crinkled in frustration. He'd made it look so easy.

I thought of the red-furred fox—pictured him speeding over woodland and meadow.

By the third moon!

"Isla? Are you out here?" The voice spoke softly and my ears flicked forward. Haiki was padding over the meadow.

I stepped out from between the ferns. "I've been . . ." My words drifted away. I didn't want to admit that I'd been practicing wa'akkir for so long, not when I had nothing to show for it. "Those dogs from the gorge appeared, and there were others."

Haiki gasped. "They traveled a long way from their territory."

"I guess they're hungry."

"And they didn't see you?"

"Siffrin distracted them and ran away. He's gone ahead to the Elders."

At the mention of the red-furred fox, Haiki licked his nose uneasily. "I'm not sure he really wanted to take us. You, perhaps . . . but not me, Simmi, or Tao. How do you know he'll be back?"

"He's just being careful." I nibbled at a burr. "He'll be back."

"All the same, I'm glad you didn't leave without us. You were gone from the den so long, I started to wonder if you had."

I glanced up. "I wouldn't do that." Haiki's ears were flat, pointing out at angles. "What is it?"

His gaze slid down to the earth. "There's something about that fox that makes me nervous. He seemed so keen to take you to the Elders, like he had some special reason . . . but he didn't want to help the skulk. Oh, I don't know. Perhaps I'm imagining it." He shook his fur. "I hope he does come back." He sounded doubtful.

"He will," I assured the gray-furred fox, ignoring a tingle of uncertainty.

Haiki took a step closer. "It's different for us," he said quietly. "The others . . . they're friendly, and they want to help. But they can't understand what we've lost." He met my gaze, his brown eyes shining. "My heart was scorched to cinders the day my family disappeared." His voice rose in a whine and he looked away. "I'd do *anything* to get my family back."

I could feel the dark knot in my chest. "I can't even see them in my thoughts. Ma, Fa, or Greatma . . ." The words died on my tongue. I had been forcing so much grief away but it hadn't gone, not really. It was always just behind me, like a shadow.

Haiki rested his muzzle against my shoulder. "We'll be all right," he murmured. "We'll keep going. One pawstep at a time, one sunrise, one nightfall. We mustn't give up."

I hadn't been close to anyone since my den was attacked. I closed my eyes and let Haiki wash my ears. His gentle touch took me back in time to the safety and warmth of a life I used to know.

Eventually, Haiki drew away. He flexed his whiskers and brightened. "Karo caught another rabbit. She's a better hunter than those dogs!"

I cocked my head, impressed.

His tail started wagging. "Let's go and eat!"

I followed Haiki back to the den. As he slipped between the nettles, I peered into the sky. The sun was floating over the meadow. There was no sign of the moon beneath its cool white glare. The gray fox was always so cheerful. But beneath his chatter, there was desperation and yearning. It was only a moment, a few words by the nettles. But we had an understanding now.

We were the same.

On the first night after Siffrin left it rained heavily, drenching the meadow. The skulk hunted till moonset but the downpour meant there was little to show for it and we all returned to the den before long.

On the second night, it was quiet and still. Karo caught a bird, and the rest of the skulk gathered earthworms and insects. By moonset, we were curled up inside, in case the Taken trod the borders of the meadow.

On the third night, the sun set in violet billows and an orange moon rose over the nettles. Most of the skulk rested in the den. Haiki curled up alone near the wall of the den, his fuzzy tail wrapped around him.

Simmi and Tao chattered nonstop about the trip to the Elder Rock. Now and then, they would turn to me to ask when Siffrin would arrive. To avoid their questions, I slunk along the tunnel and waited at the exit. My eyes grazed the dark nettles, searching for movement between the leaves. I sensed no paws racing over the grass, no trembling breath in the air.

As the moon faded to darkness, the only sounds were the click of insects and night birds screeching beneath the clouds.

Though the first hint of dawn rose over the east, Siffrin did not come.

14

We would set out for the Elder Rock without Siffrin.

A day had passed in heated conversations and half-formed plans. In the end, it was agreed that the same group would seek the Elders: me and Haiki, Simmi and Tao.

"You will have to cross the deathway," said Rupus as the skulk gathered by the nettles. "Be careful. You in particular, gray-furred fox. Where the deathway passes, the furless are found. They will want you for your coat."

Haiki swallowed, glancing at his fluffy gray brush.

"It is a shame that the messenger failed to return," the old fox sighed. "Well, that's how it is. You will have to rely on your wits."

I lowered my gaze, still stung by Siffrin's latest betrayal. He'd made me look foolish. I cursed myself angrily. *I knew he couldn't be trusted.*

Tao's tail was wagging. "Isla's going to teach us foxcraft on the journey!"

"Just karakking and slimmering," I said quickly. "I don't know the higher arts."

"It can't hurt," agreed Karo.

Flint turned to me. "Why don't you take them downstream and show them tonight? Once you're out of the meadow, you'll need to focus on your surroundings." He cocked his head at Simmi and Tao. "You can leave for the Elder Rock in the morning, armed with your new skills."

Tao's tail thrashed eagerly. "Let's go right now! I want to slimmer!"

Karo gave him a nudge with her long snout. "Be back by moonset. The Wildlands are more dangerous than ever."

"That's why you shouldn't travel by night," said Flint. "Not until you're far from the forest."

Simmi's whiskers flexed. "But how will we know which way to go?"

"I've heard the Elder Rock lies in a wood, enclosed in a circle of trees," replied Rupus.

Tao rose to his paws. "In the pine forest? That's easy enough. Come on, Isla, let's go to the stream!"

"Be patient, young fox," snapped Rupus sternly. "Use your sense. The Rock must be further than the pines."

"The messenger said it would take him three nights

to run there and back," murmured Mox. "And he knows the way."

Rupus threw Mox a sideways glance. "Shame that the brightest of the litter can't go on the journey."

Tao scowled and Simmi's ears flipped back.

"*If* Siffrin was telling the truth," Flint pointed out.

Rupus peered into the lengthening shadows. The sun was sinking into dusk. When he spoke again his voice was low. "My greatfa talked about the Elders. The entrance to their realms is said to be beautiful, surrounded by waterfalls and burnished stone. The Elder Wood faces the rising sun. You will need to cross through the pines, walking into your shadows as they lengthen. Pass the deathway and keep going until you find the place of stone and waterfalls. The Elder Wood lies beyond it."

"Did your greatfa say what the Rock looks like?" I asked, imagining dozens of stones that were all the same.

Rupus ran his tongue over his nose. "All I know is it's overlooked by a special tree. One like no other. Locate the tree and you'll find the Elders."

My ears pricked up curiously. "What kind of tree?"

"A blood-bark tree."

"*Blood-bark?*" The name made me shiver.

Rupus dipped his head in acknowledgment. "Older than the hills and valleys, its grasp on the loam is deeper than anything that grows in this meadow. The wolves believed such trees to be sacred, that they drew maa from the soil in the earliest ages of our world as Canista trod the earth. There was an abundance of maa then, before the furless arrived and chopped down the forests. So much maa, it turned the trees red."

Mox's eyes grew wide. "Canista . . . You mean the bright lights we see in the sky?"

"In a way," the old fox acknowledged. "The wolves thought the lights represented a great canid, the queen of their warlike ancestor spirits. In the stories of their Bishars, Queen Canista existed in our own world."

Mox stared at his greatfa. "Canista lived *here*?"

"That is what the wolves believed, long ago when they dwelled in the Wildlands. That Canista started life down here, before her maa rose to the sky."

Mox's tail gave a shake. "Greatfa, do you think that's true?"

Rupus snorted. "Foxes do not hold with such beliefs. Even as my greatfa shared this tale, my greatma was quick to scold him. 'A tree is just a tree,' that's what she said, and she was right. Wolves are superstitious creatures who make portents of the wind and rain. I tell you this only so you'll understand the tree's appearance."

"How does it look?" I asked.

"I have never seen it myself. Perhaps the one by the Rock is the last of its kind, though there may be one or two others scattered far across the Wildlands . . ." Rupus's tatty tail flicked up. "They are said to be great trees with a deep red bark, the color of dried blood."

Simmi was gnawing at a split claw. She rested her paw and looked at her greatfa. "Won't it look like the other trees? In a wood, how can we tell?"

Rupus sighed. "You'll know."

Flint's ears flipped back. "It's getting late. We'll talk more back in the den. Go with Isla now, and learn what fox-craft you can."

Karo stepped forward to lick Simmi and Tao on the nose. "You'll be well beyond our patch once you start your journey. We do not know what dangers lurk out there. Don't stop for anything."

Flint nuzzled her shoulder. "They aren't going till the morning." The two foxes rounded back to the den, their tails crossed.

With a playful yelp, Simmi burst toward the stream. Tao and Haiki bounded in pursuit.

Little Mox stared after them.

On impulse, I padded toward him. "Do you want to learn some foxcraft?"

He ran his tongue over his muzzle. "I can't go on the journey . . ." His crooked tail hung low.

"That doesn't matter, I could still teach you." I tapped him with an encouraging paw.

His tail started wagging. "I'd love to learn foxcraft!"

"Absolutely not," snapped one of the old vixens. She shoved her snout between us and I scrambled back. "Foxcraft takes maa, and Mox needs rest!"

She was right, of course.

Starting toward the stream, I wished I hadn't said anything. When I glanced behind me, Mox was watching, tail still wagging—even as the two old vixens ushered him back to the den.

Rupus yawned and rose to his paws. For a moment he stared at me with his small, hard eyes. Then he shook out his fur and turned away.

I wove through the long grass, following the scent trail left by Haiki, Simmi, and Tao. I thought I'd teach them to karak first. It took less maa than slimmering. I was wondering about the best way to do it when I heard voices.

My ears pricked up.

"She seems very proud of herself."

"She got it wrong about Siffrin."

The fur twitched at my hackles. It was Simmi and Tao— they were talking about me.

"That wasn't her fault," said Haiki. "How could she have known?"

Simmi snorted. "Well, she should have said sorry."

Haiki spoke with unusual force. "Isla has *nothing* to be sorry about. She isn't proud—she's brave. She's going to teach us foxcraft, and take us to the Elders. We're lucky to have her."

Warmth ran through me. It didn't matter that Siffrin hadn't come, or what Simmi and Tao thought. At least Haiki was here to stand up for me.

The young foxes didn't respond. A moment later I heard them gambol along the bank of the stream.

My tail tapped the grass. What if I tried to find the Rock on my own? Or forget the Elders: I could carry on north to the Raging River and follow the sun to the Free Lands. Maybe Pirie was there.

Simmi and Tao don't deserve my help.

My ears rotated. I remembered the rabbit Karo caught that morning, and its long, meaty leg that I'd gobbled down. Maybe they *did* deserve my help—or their skulk did at least. And I couldn't just abandon Haiki.

But there was nothing to stop me from having a little fun.

I stalked through the grass, my whiskers twitching. When I spotted Simmi up ahead, I drew in my breath.

What was seen is unseen; what was sensed becomes senseless. What was bone is bending; what was fur is air.

My heartbeat slowed and my paws flickered in and out of view. I slipped next to Simmi to hiss in her ear.

"Too proud, am I?"

Simmi shrieked and spun around. "Isla, where are you?"

I ducked into the grass, concealed in my slimmer.

"What's going on?" yelped Tao, standing with Haiki by the stream.

Simmi was craning her neck. She couldn't see me crouching a brush-length away. "It's Isla, she's right here! She must have heard us talking."

Through the syrupy gleam of the slimmer, I saw Haiki cock his head. His tail started wagging. "It's foxcraft!" he barked. "She's invisible."

Tao turned a tight circle. "We weren't serious, Isla," he called, facing the wrong direction.

I trod lightly around Simmi so I was right behind her.

"Not nice to talk about someone when they aren't there to defend themselves."

Simmi jumped, her back arching. "Stop that!" she spat. "What are you doing?"

I breathed into the downy fur of her ear. "I'm teaching you to slimmer." She snapped at the air but I dodged her teeth. "First you draw in your breath as you focus your mind on your prey." I rolled on the grass, sidling up to her other ear. "Then comes the chant." She wheeled round but I glided past her, light as a breeze.

It wasn't like back in the Graylands; I could slimmer and talk at the same time. I was *good* at it. "What was seen is unseen; what was sensed becomes senseless." Squinting through the slimmer, I saw her hackles rise. "What was bone is bending; what was fur is air."

Simmi turned in a tight circle. "Stop being creepy! Where are you?"

"Behind you!" I smacked her leg with an outstretched paw.

She flashed her teeth. "I'll get you, Isla!" I caught the hint of a whine in her voice.

"How will you do that?" I shuffled close to her puffed-up tail and gave it a sharp nip. Simmi sprang into the air with a yelp. Her voice rose as she spat: "If you want to outdo me with foxcraft, you'll have to catch me first!" She bombed downstream, launching herself through a bed of ferns. Tao ran after her, panting and barking.

They were too far away to chase, but I knew that a voice could move faster than its master. I released the slimmer to gasp great gulps of air.

I karakked, throwing my voice as I used to with Pirie, an explosion of songbirds and cawing crows. I let the sounds circle Simmi and Tao like storm clouds and splash down on them like rain. The two foxes froze, their eyes shooting up to the murky sky.

"What's happening?" Tao whimpered. "Where are all the birds coming from?"

Haiki snorted with delight, staring at the young foxes. "It's Isla. She's karakking!"

I used the karak to throw my own voice, letting it spin through the chirping and cawing. "To karak, there is no chant. You must know the call you want to mimic, know it in every detail and trill."

"Isla, is that you?" barked Simmi.

Tao shook his ears. "Her voice is bursting through my head."

I drew in my breath. *What was seen is unseen . . .*

I prowled toward them, past Haiki. His ears pricked up, as though he could sense me through my slimmer.

Simmi and Tao were less aware. They backed against each other, wide-eyed. I crept up to them easily.

"We mustn't let her catch us unprepared," Simmi hissed. "Isla's good at foxcraft."

"I'm all right."

Tao shrieked. "She's behind us!"

I threw my voice to the air once more, letting it spiral around the young foxes.

"Maybe I'm behind you. Maybe I'm in front of you. Maybe I'm *everywhere*."

Simmi stumbled against the tree. "Amazing," she murmured. She couldn't see me through the slimmer; she was bewildered by the birdcalls.

I edged closer to murmur in her ear. "Where am I now?"

She slammed against me. The shock of her contact broke the slimmer and cut across my karakking voice.

"There you are!" she panted. "You sneaky beast!"

I gave her a lick on the nose, to show there were no bad feelings.

Tao's brush was thrashing. "I can't believe you did all that!"

"Isn't she great?" yipped Haiki proudly.

The three young foxes sprang on me, batting and nipping playfully.

"Teach us!" barked Tao.

Simmi pawed my foreleg. "Yes, show us how, Isla!"

I looked overhead. Dusk had settled into a rich, dark night. The moon was the color of bone. "Sure," I murmured, rolling back on my haunches. "But you'll have to catch me first!"

We wound along the edge of the stream. Simmi and Tao took turns drawing in their breaths and spitting out crow caws. Slimmering proved to be more of a challenge. Tao struggled to slow down his heart rate and Simmi only managed a few beats before her dark coat grew visible.

"You'll get better with practice," I told them.

I was less sure about Haiki. The lowlands gray couldn't even karak. His talent seemed to lie in unmasking the arts, once I had shown him how. Blinking rapidly, he could cut through my slimmer and easily locate me. When Simmi and Flint karakked over him, he set his muzzle and ignored them.

As the others drank thirstily from the stream, I looked to Canista's Lights. Clouds blotted out the stars. Was the moon floating behind them, or had it already set?

"We should probably get back," I sighed.

Tao shook the water from his whiskers. "Greatfa won't believe our foxcraft!"

Simmi bumped up alongside him. "I can't wait to karak for Mox!"

"I'm hungry," said Tao.

Simmi nipped his ear. "We only just ate!"

Tao ran his tongue over his muzzle. "Foxcraft is hard work! Ma buried a rabbit for later, maybe she'll let us have it . . . I can practically taste it!"

Haiki licked his chops, capering beside them.

"Last one there gets the tail!" Simmi barked. She stormed across the meadow, her brush floating behind her.

"The flank is *mine*!" snarled Tao, springing after his sister.

We raced through the grass, dodging between ferns. Simmi was several brush-lengths ahead. "Me first!" she barked. "I get the rabbit!"

As I nosed into the nettles, Simmi screamed. I sprang through the foliage and stumbled to a halt. She was frozen, her ears pressed flat. Tao cowered by her side.

The smell of smoke rose in the air.

"What is it?" I breathed. Steeling myself, I padded closer.

Then I saw them: Rupus, Dexa, and Mips. The vixens were lying by the entrance to the den, deep gouges etched into their flanks. In death, they huddled together. They were of the same litter—a bond that had stayed with them to the end.

Sickness rose in my throat. Swallowing hard, I trod closer to Rupus, who was slumped alone by a bowing fern. The hint of a defiant snarl was etched in his muzzle. His round eyes glared unblinking, cloudy as ice. I gave him a nudge with my snout. His body was floppy and cool.

I shrank back with a yelp.

Simmi started toward the den. "Where are the others?"

Smoke coiled above the entrance. Its acid pelt stung my nose. "Be careful!" I hissed. I remembered the stench from my own den the night my family disappeared.

Simmi paused. "What happened?"

"The Taken," I murmured. "They've been here."

Tao whined and scrambled to Simmi's side.

"Does that mean . . . ?" Her voice faltered.

I dipped my head.

Her tail wrapped tightly around her flank. "But they left Greatfa. They killed Dexa and Mips."

I drew in my breath. "I doubt the Mage needs elderly foxes. Only foxes he can use."

Tao shook his head, bewildered. "Use for what?"

Simmi's lips peeled back. "Don't you get it? The Tailless Seer has captured Ma and Fa, and Mox too. They've been pleached—their wills have been stolen."

Tao recoiled, his muzzle trembling. "I don't believe it!"

"It's true," I said quietly. "They'll be part of the Mage's skulk now. Only foxes fit to fight."

Tao's eyes were wild. "They won't do it! Not Ma or Fa, they'll resist!"

Haiki turned away. "They won't have a choice."

Tao jutted out his snout, refusing to accept the truth. "They'll protect Mox, I know they will. He wouldn't fight, not for the Tailless Seer—not for anyone. He couldn't even kill a mouse!"

The distant cackles of the Taken rose from the Ghost Valley. I shuddered, my eyes tracing the darkness. They seized on a shape at the base of the hazel bush. At first I thought it was a rock, a mound of earth. But there was fur.

Only foxes fit to fight . . .

I blinked, dread twisting in my gut.

Mox was curled with his head on his paws. In death, he looked so small.

He might have been a cub.

15

A sharp, metallic smell clung to Mox's body. I took in the curve of his narrow back, the bones sticking out beneath his fur. The whiskers were relaxed on his gray-smudged muzzle and his eyes were closed, as if in sleep.

It was Simmi who breathed his name, her voice thick with grief. "Mox. Our own dear Mox."

Too frail to be of use to the Mage, too gentle to recruit to his army of Taken. They might have let Mox go—it wouldn't have done any harm.

Simmi and Tao threw back their heads, their voices shrill against the night. Haiki whimpered, shuffling low to the ground.

I stood still. I could feel a faint vibration against my paw pads, rising up my legs. Dark thoughts consumed me. The Mage showed no mercy for the weak, just as he attacked the strong. My family flickered before me—Ma, Fa, and Greatma—a vision that vanished into the gloom of memory.

Gekkers exploded from the border of the meadow. I whipped around to face the others. "The Taken. They're close."

Haiki threw a panicked look into the darkness. "They're coming back! We have to go."

Tao snarled with rage. "I'll kill them! Every last one of them!" He made as though to run at the Taken.

I leaped into his path. "There are too many," I hissed. "And they won't be alone. To pleach, they need a free fox— one of the Mage's inner guard. The Narral are experts in foxcraft. You wouldn't last a heartbeat."

With a chill, I remembered Siffrin's warning.

If you see a skulk of Taken, and one is a free fox, run for your life!

Tao collapsed onto his belly. He buried his muzzle in his paws with a whimper. "There's nothing we can do . . . nothing."

Simmi stood, blankly staring at the smoking den.

Another shriek of gekkers. The long grass stirred near the hazels. The Taken must have heard the yowls. They were coming back.

Haiki dropped to Tao's side, nudging him with his snout. "Come with us," he soothed. "We'll find the Elders. That's something. Don't give up . . ." Tao rose on quivering legs.

He let Haiki lead him toward the nettles. Simmi followed blindly, her fur on end.

As I slipped behind them, through the nettles, the shadowy figures arrived at the den. I paused, concealed in dense foliage—seeking out the Narral.

It wasn't hard to identify him. Among the red-eyed Taken stalked a fox with the frame of a dog. He was nothing like Karka—there was no power in his squat limbs. He looked almost comical: his auburn fur was greasy and his ears stuck out at strange angles. His round chest gave him a clumsy gait, while his blunt snout made him look foolish. But there was cunning in his eyes.

We ran through the meadow, along the path of the stream. Our pace didn't slow until the land curved up toward the forest and we reached the first cluster of pines. A sliver of light touched the eastern horizon, the first sign that the long night had broken.

We rested briefly. Simmi and Tao curled together, and Haiki lay by my side. I longed for sleep but my mind was a nest of wasps.

The Great Snarl was rigid, with its walls and endless graystone. In the Wildlands, everything moved. Branches fanned the wind, bobbing with new buds. Grasses shivered and birds dived overhead. The forest was alive with chirping and buzzing—with hissing voices and hooded eyes.

We set out again as the sun rose higher, edging around the tree-lined hill where Siffrin had fought the coyote chief.

Siffrin . . . Why hadn't he returned? What if something had happened to him?

Simmi and Tao were up ahead, walking side by side, tails dragging behind them. Haiki padded toward me and gave me a lick on the nose. "It was a tough night. How are you?"

"I'm all right." I glanced at Simmi and Tao. "I wish we could have done something. If only Siffrin had come back."

Haiki looked at me warily. "I've been thinking about that."

My whiskers twitched. "Go on."

His voice was soft. "Don't you think it's strange how he left when he did? Just before the den was attacked."

"You can't mean . . ." A chill ran along my back. I thought of the red-furred fox. Siffrin was arrogant, dismissive. Selfish, even. But he was no friend of the Mage.

"I can't stop thinking about it," said Haiki. "All the promises he made. I wonder if he ever meant to take us to the Elders. Maybe he just said that to keep you happy."

My ears flicked back. "Why would he do that?"

Haiki shook his ears. "I don't know. I just have a bad feeling . . . I've had one since he arrived that night, bringing the coyotes with him. Who is Siffrin? I mean, who is he really?"

A tremor of color crossed my mind, of red against red, a vision from maa-sharm. Marshlands, a stalking vixen, a tiny cub at the edge of a forest. A creeping yellow mist and the stench of decay.

I blinked and the image disappeared. Bars of white sunshine leaped between the trees. I caught a familiar sound—the yawning hum of manglers. So it was true: the deathway cut deep into the Wildlands. Even here, the furless were never far away.

"Be careful," I called to Simmi and Tao. No one answered. My ears pricked up. "Where are the others?"

I picked my way through the bracken, Haiki by my side. Shards of light broke overhead. The pines were further apart now, the ground growing rocky. "Simmi? Tao?"

Tao appeared from behind a tree. I was surprised to find him bright-eyed. His tail even gave a small wag. "Isla, Haiki, come quickly! Simmi's found an amazing hunk of meat!"

Simmi was standing by the trunk of a pine. She looked up excitedly as we approached. "You won't believe it. I thought it would be hard to catch our own food, but I just found this! It smells *so* good."

I peered over her shoulder. Tao was right—there was a huge hunk of pinkish meat lying on the grass, boneless and hairless, ready to eat. The spicy-sweet smell was intoxicating. I looked around. Who had left this kill? It couldn't have been here long. As I licked my whiskers and craned my head, a flash of ginger fur reflected back at me.

"What's that?" The meat was encased in two wire loops, and rising from each were serrated teeth.

"It's all right," Simmi assured me. "I saw that, but it isn't moving." She raised a forepaw toward the meat as Haiki and Tao watched eagerly.

Why would anyone abandon a slab of meat in the forest? Why would they lodge it between wire loops?

The deathway hummed nearby. I thought of the jagged world of the furless, a land of sharp edges and shiny walls. The snatchers with their cages; the beast dens with their endless bars.

"Leave it!" I hissed and Simmi quailed, backing away from the meat. Haiki and Tao stared at me in surprise.

I was sorry to alarm them. The meat was the first thing that had lifted the young foxes' spirits. I looked about, found a wooden stick, and lifted it in my mouth. I slid the stick toward the meat and gave it a prod. Instantly, the wire jaws sprang to life, smashing together violently. The wooden stick snapped in two.

Simmi gasped. "That could have been my leg!"

Tao looked sickened. "How did you know?"

"The furless," I murmured. "I grew up among them."

Haiki backed away from the wire jaws, which remained clamped together. "But why?" he whimpered. "Why would they do it?"

How could I answer him? There was no "why."

Wariness hung over us. Simmi and Tao were somber again, and Haiki paused often to sniff the air. Perhaps he remembered the furless with the stick. Small creatures scratched around the forest floor. A mouse scampered beneath the trunk of a tree. A squirrel darted along a branch. None of us tried to hunt. It felt safer to keep moving.

Steadily, the groan of the deathway grew louder. Simmi and Tao exchanged glances, their tails dragging behind them. Haiki fell into step by my side. Nobody spoke.

Eventually, it came into view—a great, gray expanse dividing the land.

Crossing the deathway would be harder than I'd imagined. It had swelled to a giant sprawl, with manglers zooming back and forth on either side. While they moved more quickly than in the Great Snarl, I noticed that the manglers were less frequent. It was a matter of choosing your moment and running across.

The challenge was convincing the others.

Haiki backed from the edge of the deathway, his fur on end. "There must be another way."

"We could edge around it," agreed Simmi, her ears pinned back.

But the graystone paving stretched out in both directions, as far as the eye could see. Even if we found the end, the detour was bound to add days to our journey.

"What if it goes all the way to the Raging River?" I said.

Reluctantly, the three young foxes lined up alongside me at the bank of the deathway. The roar of passing manglers was deafening. I had to bark to be heard. "Get ready to run with me as fast as you can. All right?"

They yipped in agreement.

"Not before I say," I warned them. My ears pricked forward and I watched the deathway. Three sleek manglers raced by in one direction, another speeding further along the graystone the other way. They seemed oblivious to us, but I knew they wouldn't pause if we crossed their path. We would have to be quick.

After a while the graystone became almost quiet. I could hear the wind whistling between the pines. I caught the distant grumble of a mangler but I saw no sign of one on the deathway.

"Now!" I barked. I started to run. Tao and Simmi were by my side, racing blindly over the deathway. When I reached the middle, I threw my head over my shoulder. Haiki was just behind us. "Hurry!"

The growl of the mangler was quickly rising. The graystone trembled beneath the weight of its thick, round paws. Soon it would appear on the horizon. I broke over the deathway, pounding the graystone until I reached the other side. Simmi and Tao dropped alongside me on the grass, yipping and panting for breath.

"We did it! We survived the deathway!"

"It's *so* big! I wish Ma and Fa could have seen it . . ."

I stretched out my forepaws, relieved to have the deathway behind us. It was worse out here in the Wildlands. It wasn't only that the manglers were faster, that the graystone was wider. Here, surrounded by trees, its aggression seemed more startling.

My head snapped up. "Where's Haiki?"

The long-furred fox was frozen in the middle of the graystone. He cowered, tail wrapped around his flank, refusing to go any further. "Haiki, what are you doing?" I howled. "You need to run this way as fast as you can!"

"I *can't*!" he cried. "The manglers will get me!" Even from this distance I could see his body quaking. My eyes swept the deathway and my gut clenched with fear. A mangler was rushing into view. Its bright red shell was shiny like a beetle's. It gave a deafening roar when it saw Haiki.

Tao and Simmi had turned to the deathway, screaming at Haiki until their voices cracked. "Hurry, Haiki, run this way!"

Haiki stared at them, his eyes wild with terror, his paws sticking firmly to the graystone.

16

I couldn't watch as the mangler screamed into Haiki's path. I clenched my eyes shut, my head in my paws.

"What's he doing?" gasped Tao.

I looked up to see Haiki bolting toward the forest. He had ducked away from the mangler just in time. A moment later another sped over the graystone. Haiki darted a few steps forward, a few steps back.

"This way!" I howled. I wasn't sure if he'd hear me above the roar of the mangler. Simmi and Tao were barking in unison, "This way! This way!"

Haiki started running toward us. The mangler was speeding over the deathway, its beetle-shell exterior as gray as Haiki's fur. Inside I saw two watchful furless. One raised her forepaws to her face. As Haiki broke before the mangler it swerved away, careening at a furious angle. It seemed set to spring over the far bank of the deathway but righted itself and leaped forward. One of the furless was focused ahead but the other spun around, eyes wide as the mangler rumbled away.

Haiki sprinted, his ears flat, until he reached us on the far bank. He collapsed against the grass. Simmi and Tao assaulted him with friendly nips.

"What were you thinking?" I snapped, licking his ears.

"I was sure that was the end of you!" whimpered Tao.

Haiki was shaking from nose to tail. "Those manglers . . . They were so much faster . . ."

I licked my fur clean of the dust from the deathway. "Are there manglers in the lowlands?"

Haiki stretched his back legs. "I mean they're faster than I expected. Even a coyote can't run like that!" He cringed away from the bank and I rolled onto my paws to follow him. There was a hedgerow, and beyond it a field. We padded closer, snouts low. Every time a mangler passed, the ground quivered beneath our paws. Their foul breath licked the surrounding grass. I longed to get back to the cover of trees.

Simmi padded next to us. "The sun is moving over the deathway. We need to go in that direction." She tipped her nose toward the field.

We shuffled beneath the hedgerow and along the tangling grass at the edge of the field. Slim plants grew in neat grooves. Rigid, trapped . . . evidence of the furless. I picked up pace. The sooner we reentered woodland, the safer we would be. At least the light was on our side. I didn't want to be out in the Wildlands after the sun set. Would the Mage's skulk venture this far? I couldn't be sure. The deathway wouldn't stop them—if the Mage ordered them to cross it, I knew they would.

Would the Taken dare approach the Elders?

I remembered what Siffrin had told me about the shana.

It's a ring of maa that the Elders weave around the Elder Rock in a secret ritual called "shana-sharm." Without it, the Mage might attack any time.

We'd be safe once we reached the Elder Rock.

Unless . . .

Unless we can't cross the shana either. What if the Elders wouldn't let us pass without Siffrin? I glanced at my companions. Haiki had recovered, his gray tail wagging as he padded between Simmi and Tao. The two young foxes walked with somber purpose.

I wondered if I should mention the shana. Was it only there to keep out the Mage's forces, the so-called pleached foxes? Or could it block entry to everyone?

My ears pricked up. A rabbit bounced across the field and stopped to rest along the rows of green plants, its small nose twitching. Another paused to groom its long ears.

Tao had paused by my side.

Simmi ran her tongue over her muzzle. "Maybe we should try to catch one."

Haiki stared across the field with longing. "They're too far away."

We'd eaten not long before leaving the den to practice foxcraft. Still, my belly growled. I'd never caught a rabbit. "We could slimmer to get closer."

The young foxes turned to me.

"Slimmering is hard," said Simmi. "Will you show us how to use it to catch a rabbit?"

"Oh yes, show us," agreed Tao.

I scanned the field. The rabbit was grooming its ears. It was further away than I would have liked—I'd have to hold the slimmer for a while. "There might be furless nearby."

Tao cocked his head. "I don't see any. We'll keep a lookout."

I didn't like to admit that I'd never caught a rabbit before. "It's all the way across the field . . ."

"If anyone can do it, you can, Isla." Haiki's tail was thumping the earth.

My whiskers flexed. I couldn't back out now. I started stalking along the neat green plants. The rabbit blinked in my direction. I slowed down, started chanting. "What was seen is unseen; what was sensed becomes senseless. What was bone is bending; what was fur is air."

My breathing eased; my heartbeat slowed. Through the glaze of my slimmer I saw the rabbit resume grooming. As I wove between the plants, I realized that I'd gotten it wrong. I wouldn't be able to hold the slimmer long enough to catch the rabbit. Simmi, Tao, and Haiki were watching from the edge of the field. I would disappoint them, embarrass myself . . .

My focus waned and my heartbeat quickened. To still my mind, I silently repeated the chant.

What was bone is bending; what was fur is air . . .

I started forward again, my paws moving silkily over the ground. The rabbit was no more than a glow in the distance. I stopped worrying that it was too far away. I didn't fret about anything. Within the melting ease of the slimmer, I relaxed.

As I shifted toward the center of the field, I sensed a shiver of movement. A small ball of light drifted to my side and lingered there. Through the faintest quiverings of the soil, I felt a rapid heartbeat. The creature had stumbled into my path. Perhaps it guessed I was close, but it couldn't know where. It squeaked and skipped a few paces. It didn't sound like a rabbit.

A sweet, delicious flavor filled my nostrils. In an instant, I broke from the slimmer, pouncing on the creature and throwing it down. As my eyes refocused, I saw something that looked like a large squirrel, with small ears and a bushy tail. It squeaked frantically as Simmi, Tao, and Haiki burst over the field. The rabbit spooked and ran. I didn't care: I'd caught a creature that was almost as large as a rabbit . . . and as tasty by the smell that rose from its golden fur.

"A ground squirrel!" yipped Tao.

As Simmi gave it a quick death, Haiki looked on with awe. "That was incredible!" he breathed. "Almost as though it jumped into your path. You make skill seem effortless! No one would guess it was *foxcraft*."

"Now us!" said Simmi.

"Yes, please," whined Tao. "We want to try slimmering again."

"All right," I said. "We'll give it a go. But first, let's eat."

They bounced around me, licking my muzzle. After the shame of stealing the skulk's cache, the delight at sharing my kill was dizzying. Even more so now, when it lightened the mood.

I took a quick look over the field. The truth was that the unfortunate creature really had jumped into my path— that I'd lacked the breath to stalk as far as the rabbit. But it would have run if it had seen me. *So the slimmer did count for something,* I assured myself. Even if it had been more luck than skill.

Bright days in the Wildlands didn't last long. We practiced slimmering until the orange sun hung low in the sky. The others weren't ready to hunt yet, but they were getting better. Simmi could disappear from view for several beats at a time, moving quite quickly while invisible. Tao had also improved now that he could control his breathing.

Haiki had given up on foxcraft, but he'd bark every time the others slimmered, knowing exactly where they were.

"That's useful too," I assured him.

"Useful how?" he asked dejectedly.

I thought a moment. "If one of the Narral crosses your path, you'll be able to spot their foxcraft. That gives you a kind of power."

"You mean those foxes loyal to the Tailless Seer?" Haiki shuddered. "I hope I never cross paths with them."

"I hope I do," snarled Simmi. "I'm going to make the Elders teach me the higher arts. I'll practice and practice until I'm a master of foxcraft. Then I'll track down the Narral, and the Seer himself, and I'll rip them to strips so they can't pleach anyone else."

"Me too," hissed Tao. "The Narral are worse than the Taken—they *choose* to do the Seer's killing. I'm going to hunt them, every last one. I don't care if I die trying."

I dipped my head. I couldn't blame them.

I felt the same.

We continued across the field, then along the edges of another. I was glad when I spotted the tops of green pines crowding around a pasture. As we slid beneath their shade, the light that glanced between the branches glowed deep orange.

Dusk settled, with its distinctive sounds and smells. Tiny insects buzzed in clouds, flickers of transparent wings. The ground smelled fresh and damp, though no rain fell from the sky.

The hum of evening was closing in.

"Can you feel that?" asked Simmi, her voice a whisper over the whirr of insects.

My ears rotated. "Feel what?"

"A tingle against your paw pads?"

I paused, looking down at the ground. Now that she mentioned it, there was a faint sensation rising from the soil. I had felt something similar back in the meadow, though only for a moment.

Simmi cocked her head. "I thought you would, though you're from the Graylands. You know, because of your sensitive maa."

"Malinta's close," explained Tao. "You'll feel it fading and growing stronger with the next moon. But that's nothing—wait till we reach the gloaming."

"I don't feel anything," said Haiki in a small voice. "I remember the gloaming, but nothing much about malinta. My head's a bit of a muddle sometimes . . ."

Simmi gave him a reassuring nudge. "You'll feel it sooner or later."

I thought about maa, and the mysterious power of the earth that had once reached out like a beating heart and woven me close to my brother. Blinking up into shards of orange light, I sensed his presence. "I'll catch up," I told the others.

They looked at me curiously.

"I need to be alone for a while. Don't worry, I'll find you."

Haiki peered into the shadows. "Before it gets dark?"

"Before it gets dark," I agreed. I watched him pad after Simmi and Tao. He glanced back, once, and I blinked at him. I waited until the three foxes had disappeared beneath the pines. Then I trod a wide circle, trying to find a suitable spot. I settled on a slim beam of light. Between the pines, the orange sky had deepened to red.

"Pirie?" I murmured. "Pirie, are you there?"

Insects buzzed around my ears. I shook my head, my tail thumping in agitation. I closed my eyes and tried to ignore them.

"Pirie, can you hear me?"

The faint tingle in my paw pads grew stronger. It tickled against my claws, as though the earth was responding to my call. The buzz of insects faded and the forest grew still. Only the softest sound touched my ears, a voice that might have been a breath of wind.

Isla, is that you?

My tail gave an excited wag. "Pirie, I thought I'd lost you! You've been so quiet."

It's harder now.

"Why, what's changed? What's happened to you?"

I don't know . . . my mind is tangled. To reach you like this takes concentration, but I am rarely myself.

My tail stiffened. "Has someone hurt you?"

There was a pause. *I'm not in pain.*

His response didn't soothe me. "Where are you?"

In darkness . . . deep . . . I cannot escape.

A chill ran through me. "I'll help you. But first, I need to know where you are. Can you describe it? Or how you get there?"

I don't know, Isla. I can't say more. I'm scared for you.

"Scared for *me*? But I'm safe."

Stay safe, Isla. That is all that matters. Stay free.

Pirie's voice sank with the breeze and the tingle dulled against my paw pads. I reached out to him but he had retreated where I could not follow.

A shot of anger cut through me, sharp and unexpected. "Why are you running from me?" I growled. "What sort of game are you playing? I've come so far in search of you, Pirie. I won't give up on you, no matter what you say!"

He was acting like he didn't want to be found. His words echoed in my mind.

I'm scared for you.

"Don't try to protect me, Pirie. I don't need your help! I don't need *anyone's* help."

My eyes flicked open. The red light had gone and the world around me had lapsed into night. Darkness swelled beneath the pines. I shook my head, confused. Which direction had the others gone? I'd promised Haiki I would join them before dark, but it had come so suddenly.

I padded toward a large trunk, sniffing its base. Had the foxes passed this way? "Haiki? Simmi?" I threw back my head and barked.

Instead of a fox's voice, I heard the *Kaah! Kaah!* of ravens.

Flesh-eating birds.

The fur stiffened at the back of my neck.

My ears pricked up. I thought I'd caught the distant hum of the deathway. I started to trot in the other direction, into the deepening forest. My paws stepped lightly over the loam as my eyes scanned the world ahead. Between the branches the gray of cloud cover banished the stars.

"Tao?"

With a tremor of relief, I picked up the young male's scent. I let out a deep breath. They had passed this way not long ago. I tracked the odor, my muzzle low. As I turned beyond the trunk of a pine, my whiskers bristled. My nostrils stung and I recoiled, a rank taste catching the back of my tongue.

The stench of decay.

A ripple of fear ran along my back. A strange groan rose from the soil. Not the faint, pleasing tingle of malinta's approach, but the croak of a garbled curse.

In the crumbs of light beneath the branches, a yellow mushroom with purple speckles shunted its head through the soil. Another appeared alongside it, less than a brush-length from my paw.

It was then that I heard the thump of pawsteps, loping through the wood. Foxes, but not Haiki, Simmi, or Tao. Six or seven adults, perhaps a whole skulk. When I turned I saw their silhouettes against the stiff-backed pines.

The Taken have found me.

Their red-rimmed eyes were glowing.

17

It was too late to slimmer—the Taken had seen me. I recognized the bony vixen from the Ghost Valley. At the head of the pack, she gave a shrill gekker. The other foxes echoed her call. Up in the branches, birds flapped frantically. Down on the forest floor, small creatures scurried.

But the Taken weren't after them.

I shot between two pines, racing into the night. My pulse drummed in my ears. I could feel the thud of their paws on the soil. I cut between trees at a frantic zigzag, doing my best to throw them off course. It didn't work: a glance over my shoulder revealed a mass of dark bodies. They were gaining on me with each step.

"This way!" hissed Tao. He was crouching behind the trunk of a tree. Together we sprinted in the darkness.

Haiki and Simmi were hiding in some shrubs. When they saw us, they started to run. The ground sloped uphill and the tree cover grew denser. I struggled to keep up with the others, my legs shorter than theirs. The wind picked up, blowing back my fur. Panic thrummed at the base of my ears. The Taken were downwind of us. They would smell us, could easily track us. I found myself wondering what Siffrin would do. But of course, he had wa'akkir—the precious fox-craft he wouldn't share.

I am the fur that ruffles your back. I am the twist and shake of your tail . . .

I willed my paws to change into those of a mighty dog. I watched for slanted claws rising from the small pads.

The chant did nothing.

Rage welled inside me, giving me speed that I didn't know I had. I surged forward, keeping pace with Tao. My forepaws tingled as they thumped the ground. Was it malinta, calling to me? The tree cover parted. The clouds webbed and split, revealing a velvety sky. An icy white moon glowed overhead. Beyond it I caught the twinkle of stars. It gave me the strength to go on.

But as we wheeled around a tree trunk the earth fell away, pitching down to a ravine.

"Careful!" yelped Simmi, slamming to a halt. We piled up behind her, gasping for breath. The drop was steep—too far, too dark, to see what lay below. Pines clung to the tumbling soil, bunching in a cluster down below. We would have to edge our way along their arching roots.

Simmi was the first to launch herself over the top of the ravine. She spread out her paws, sliding down to the next tree trunk and smacking into it awkwardly. Catching her breath, she stepped out from behind the tree and started sliding again. Her foreleg tripped on a loose root.

"Simmi!" Tao was darting toward her, his tail flying behind him.

"I'm all right!" She was hugging the next tree with her forepaws as he came crashing after her.

Haiki stood in a pool of moonlight between the trees. He turned to me, his brown eyes glinting. "This is dangerous, Isla—I don't think we should go that way."

I could hear the Taken striding through the forest. What else could we do? "We'll be careful," I told him, though I wasn't sure how. Ears flat, I pounced downhill. I smacked onto my belly, tumbling faster than I'd expected. Swinging my flank around and digging my paws into the soil, I managed to steady my pace and regain some control. A moment later, I hit a tree, yelping with pain as the hard trunk bit into my leg. I looked up at Haiki, who was frozen at the top of the ravine.

His gray fur was fuzzy against the light. His anxious gaze was fixed on me. He couldn't have seen the looming shadow.

"Haiki, look out!"

Two red-eyed foxes rose behind him, a bony vixen and a short-haired male. Haiki started and cowered from their path. The pleached foxes were moving so quickly that they tumbled over the edge of the ravine. The bony vixen pounced past Haiki with outstretched paws. The short-haired male lurched between two trees and started rolling. I heard the crack of bones as they fell into the darkness of the clustering pines.

My stomach flipped as I strained to see what had happened. Simmi and Tao were clinging to a lower trunk. Remembering the other Taken, I looked up to the top of the ravine. A series of pointed ears rose in silhouette. Their eyes pulsed red. Together, they lifted their forelegs and started forward.

The Mage is telling them what to do!

Where was Haiki?

It was at that moment I heard his voice, gekkering from further in the forest.

"This way!" he yelped. "Catch me if you can!"

The Taken's heads swung around in unison.

My jaw dropped. I expected recklessness from Siffrin, but not from the fearful gray-furred fox. I wanted to call him, to beg him to stop, but he was already too far away. I could hear his gekkers over the forest as the Taken charged after him.

"This way," hissed Tao. "There are rocks, and what looks like a passage."

I followed his gaze. At the edge of the ravine was a series of boulders. Silvery flecks in the stone glittered under moonlight. "But Haiki is up there alone," I gasped.

Simmi raised her muzzle but didn't meet my eye. "We couldn't get back there if we tried."

I couldn't believe they were ready to give up on him so quickly. I pressed against the trunk of the pine and pushed myself back up the incline. I'd only managed half a brushlength when I slipped in a tumble of earth, smacking my bruised leg. I nipped the trunk angrily. Simmi was right. At this angle, it was impossible to climb.

"Over here." Tao was edging very carefully across the incline, his paws splayed for balance. His brush swung back and forth, helping him stay upright. He crept through the darkness, resting beneath me at the next tree. As he pushed away from the trunk, out onto the steep ravine once more, Simmi started after him. She reached the trunk he had left behind, just as he paused at the next one. Stalking low, they crossed beneath me toward the glittering rocks.

I strained my ears. I could no longer hear Haiki's gekkers or the footfall of the Taken. They must have retreated into the wood. How fast was Haiki? I remembered how he'd cowered on the deathway. Could he really outrun the Taken?

I tried to hang on to this thought as I edged beyond the tree, shifting gradually paw by paw over the crumbling ground. My ears flipped back. Had I heard a distant yelp from the wood? Or was it only the hoot of a bird?

"Isla?"

Simmi and Tao had reached the rocks and were waiting for me.

I started to move again. For a moment I lost my footing and tottered as dirt toppled between my paws. My teeth snapped at an exposed root. I clamped down on it, catching my breath. More slowly, I reached out a forepaw and carefully shifted my weight. Step by step, tail juddering behind me, I managed to make it to the rocks.

Simmi and Tao met me with whines, licking my whiskers and washing my ears. I greeted them back.

It wasn't a yelp, I told myself sharply. *Just the call of a bird.*

The rocks sprang out of the edge of the ravine in sharp disks. The gaps between them were just about large enough for a fox to edge through, but we had to move with care. Darkness skirted the rock formation, deep and foreboding. Beneath it lay a depthless fall.

Tao shuffled forward, keeping his body low.

Simmi paused to look back at me. "Aren't you coming?" Her eyes were shiny globes.

I peered along the rock wall, but couldn't see beyond to the top of the ravine. "What about Haiki?"

An explosion of gekkers rose in the distance. Simmi was firm. "We can't wait."

We slipped along the path between the rocks, careful not to stray too close to the edge. In time, the sound of running water filled the air, though all I could see before me was the sweep of Simmi's brush and the expanding blackness of the night. We crawled up over jagged mounts and padded warily downhill. The layered rocks seemed to run forever along the outside track of the woodland, rising into ragged cliffs.

Tao turned back to me and Simmi. "I can hear a stream up ahead, or maybe it's a few streams. It's hard to tell. I don't know where the sound's coming from."

My ears twisted. Tao was right, there seemed to be more than one source of water, but as I tried to fix on the spluttering fizz, I grew confused. Was the water up ahead, or trickling behind us? It bubbled in my ears, above, below . . . I gave my head a shake. The sensation reminded me of how I'd felt when Siffrin had slimmered and karakked at the same time, turning himself invisible and throwing his voice in a tumbling cascade. I felt giddy and light on my paws.

"It's strange," Simmi murmured.

My paw was tingling against the rock. I gave it a shake and flicked back my ears, trying to dull the sound of water. It was as though the stream was in my mind.

"We may be safer waiting until dawn." I squinted over the edge of the rocks but saw no sign of the moon, no hint of daybreak over the horizon. "One wrong move . . ."

Simmi dipped her head. "I don't want to go any further until we can see where we are."

"And if we wait awhile, Haiki might catch up."

Simmi and Tao didn't respond to this, letting my words hang against the fizz of the invisible water.

Simmi's ears pricked up. "Isla, what were you doing earlier . . . when you wanted us to go on ahead?"

"I . . . Oh, nothing." I didn't want to talk about gerra-sharm. My moments with Pirie were private.

"It's only . . ." Simmi glanced at her brother. "Those pleached foxes arrived just after."

I stiffened. What was she trying to say? "I didn't call them! Do you think I'm crazy?"

Tao's voice was soft. "But they came. They seem to follow you around. I'm not accusing you of anything, I just wondered."

I growled defensively. "They probably stalk the woodland." My whiskers twitched as I remembered what Pirie had murmured as he'd drifted beyond my reach.

I can't say more. I'm scared for you.

The power of gerra-sharm had unraveled, leaving me alone in the forest. But I hadn't been alone for long.

My mind wound back to the Ghost Valley. I'd paused to call to Pirie as we'd rounded the base of the mountain. Again, his warning rang in my ears.

Turn back. Don't look. It isn't safe.

Moments later, the Taken had arrived.

Simmi and Tao were staring at me. "What is it?"

My jaw fell slack. "The Taken came after I was lost in thought . . . lost in foxcraft."

Tao cocked his head. "What type of foxcraft?"

"Gerra-sharm," I said. "The most private meeting of minds." But what if someone else could hear our thoughts? I was horrified by the possibilities. Were the Mage's forces spying on us?

It isn't safe.

Pirie's warning hung in the air, sinking beyond the bewildering fizz of water.

The bite of the dark crept under my fur and I drew my tail around me. "I think you're right," I said at last. "I used gerra-sharm in the forest." My throat was dry as dust. "I never meant to summon the Taken. I didn't think they would come. I don't know anything about the Elders, and hardly any foxcraft. Why would they look for me?" But Karka had looked, hadn't she? Her eerie skulk had stalked the Graylands. Using me to find Pirie. Had I endangered him too?

Simmi's eyes were hard. "Did you try this . . . this *gerra-sharm* in our meadow? Did you use it last night?"

Her meaning struck me. "No!" I yelped. "Not since the Ghost Valley." My voice quivered with shame. "Though I tried once or twice."

Simmi and Tao exchanged wary glances.

My ears were flat against my head. "Please believe me. I didn't call the Taken last night!"

Tao let out a long breath. "It's too dark to go any further. We'll have to wait it out till dawn and work out what to do then."

I dropped my muzzle, feeling sick to my stomach. "I've been such a fool."

Simmi looked away. "You're a cub from the Graylands. You may have lots of maa, but you've never been taught how to use it safely. I guess you didn't think about what you were doing."

Tao was more forgiving. "She didn't mean any harm."

"It doesn't matter what I meant," I whined bitterly. "I brought the Taken close to your den. I led them through the wood. Siffrin warned me about foxcraft but I never guessed it could be used against me . . . Haiki tried to protect us, and now he's gone."

Shame crept along my fur. Siffrin was right, I lacked the maturity for the higher arts. I didn't understand foxcraft and had wielded it without a second thought. The full realization of what I'd done began to dawn on me. I had brought disaster upon my friends. I had allowed the

Mage's forces to trail us through my thoughts. I had endangered Pirie.

It's all my fault.

My head sank onto my paws. Against the hush of falling water, Tao and Simmi curled next to each other, slowly drifting to sleep. I stared out into the darkness. I didn't think I would ever sleep again. But in time, my thoughts unraveled and I pictured waterfalls falling around me. Rainbow colors danced in their tiny bubbles. A fox dived in and out of them, his mottled coat growing dappled with water.

When I opened my eyes, the fox had disappeared. I didn't dare to call for him anymore. My brother felt close, but more out of reach than ever.

Light hung over a slate horizon. We must have been exhausted; we had slept through the sunrise. Giddily, I rose to my paws. Simmi and Tao were fast asleep by my side, their tails crossed. The rocks were touched by silver flecks that sparkled as I moved. I crept to the edge and peered over. Cliffs surrounded us, so steep that the land below was a smudge of green from the tops of distant pines. Waterfalls tumbled at angles to the rockshafts, crashing and bubbling and gushing along the drop.

My eyes widened in wonder. We had reached the entrance to the Elders' realms, the place of waterfalls and burnished stone.

I turned back to gaze over the path we had taken. Slightly above us, across a craggy rock, a slim sheath of water slipped down in soft waves. Through its gossamer light I caught a flicker of movement. Someone was creeping over the rocks, light on his paws, a mass of dark fur. I opened my jaws to raise the alarm but no sound emerged from my throat. The fizz of water was tumbling around me, seizing my tongue, drowning my thoughts.

18

I hissed, rising onto my paws. My back arched instinctively, smacking against the low roof of rock. As the figure emerged through the waterfall I took a step back, then gasped in amazement. His fur was slick and darkened with water. It made him look older and leaner, somehow tougher, not the shy and youthful fox that I knew him to be.

"Haiki . . . is it really you?"

His tail lashed as he hurried toward me.

"Careful!" I warned. The rock path was narrow, ending in steep drops and further waterfalls.

Simmi and Tao yelped, wide-awake. The four of us touched noses, nipping and growling playfully.

My eyes trailed over Haiki's sodden coat. There was no sign of injury. "I can't believe you're safe!"

"What happened?" asked Tao. "How did you escape the pleached foxes?"

Haiki shook out his fur. "At first, I wanted them to follow me so they'd leave you alone." He met my gaze. "I didn't expect them to run as fast as they did. There were so many of them! I raced back through the forest, almost to where it began. I hid behind trees and rolled in dirt to disguise my scent. I knew I had to wait it out. At the first hint of dawn, they gave up and retreated . . . I don't know where, or why they suddenly appeared like that. I ran flat out until I reached the cliffs."

I hung my head. "I called them. I'm to blame."

"That can't be right." Haiki spoke with assurance. "You would never call the Taken!"

"Not on purpose . . . it has something to do with gerra-sharm."

"What's that?"

"Foxcraft," I murmured. "A way to connect with another fox through your thoughts. I was trying to speak to my brother. But the Mage must have heard me. I never imagined . . ."

Haiki let out a slow breath. "Is that what you were doing before the Ghost Valley? I heard you talking to yourself."

"I was talking to Pirie. Then the Taken came."

"They stalk that valley," Simmi pointed out graciously. "They might have been there anyway."

I turned back to her. "But they appeared all at once. They knew we were there."

Haiki padded closer and nuzzled my shoulder. "You couldn't have realized. It isn't your fault. None of this is your fault."

We picked our way through the narrow shafts of rock. This drew us near to the edge, where waterfalls streaked over the ashen cliffs, lighting them with rainbows. The air was sweet and tinkled gently from the many small streams. Colors sparkled through the water. Butterflies wove patterns under their arches, their bright wings glittering against the watery light.

The rocks morphed in the sun, turning translucent, as though we were stepping on colored air. We passed under an arch of stone, where a spider had spun a web. Tiny dewdrops dangled off its delicate frame, each a bead of red, yellow, orange, and green. Each lit with purple and blue. I blinked, seeing rainbows wherever I looked.

The sounds and colors made me sleepy. I paused, my paw pads tingling.

"When is malinta?" I asked.

"Soon," said Tao vaguely.

I plodded behind him.

"I'm tired," yawned Haiki. "Maybe we should have a nap."

A waterfall tumbled ahead of us. The rainbow colors dazzled my eyes and I squeezed them shut. A thought sharpened in my mind. "Malinta . . . It must be a time of great maa."

"Yes," said Simmi, ambling up ahead. "Enough to make the flowers bloom. Though not as much as the gloaming."

A memory was nagging at me, something about malinta, but the whispering waterfalls washed it away. "The Elders," I murmured, opening my eyes. "How do they live?"

Simmi gave me a strange look. "What do you mean?"

"They must eat, sleep . . . Do they share the kill?"

"They aren't a skulk," said Haiki, padding up behind me.

"What does it matter?" muttered Tao.

We strayed deeper through the rocks. They rose and descended like stepping-stones. The staggering drop was hidden behind the waterfalls. Only the occasional flash of greenery hinted at the land below.

The tingling in my paws grew stronger. A strange beat rose from the rocks.

It does matter, I thought. *But why?*

Ahead of me, Tao reached toward a butterfly with his forepaw, angling dangerously close to the edge.

"Be careful," I hissed, and he shrank back. He gave his head a quick shake. "You're right, that was too close."

We fell into silence, treading a narrow path as the sun rose higher in the sky. The air tinkled with the song of the waterfalls. I sank into daydreams, remembering my patch back in the Graylands. I pictured it as I'd never seen it, bursting with the buds and flowers of malinta. Memory blurred with reality and I sighed happily.

Time drained away on the rocks. Shadows lengthened, springing over the stone to be gobbled up by waterfalls.

The fur tingled along my back. "What is this place?" A strange fatigue sank through my paws. I might have slept here, just where I stood. I might have stayed here forever. When I blinked my eyes, I could still see rainbows.

"It's beautiful," murmured Haiki. I followed his gaze. Up ahead, where Simmi was walking, the rock rose into an arch. I caught the outline of a spider's web. Each delicate thread dangled with tiny beads of water.

Haiki's ears were flat. "We've been here before."

Tao looked at him.

"The web . . ."

My whiskers twitched. "But we can't have. We've been walking forward the whole time, along the edge of the cliff."

Simmi sniffed the glittering rock. "I'm not sure . . ."

Haiki's tail curled around his flank. "There's something wrong."

I gazed across one of the waterfalls. "It's so peaceful here. The water bubbles and chimes like a song."

Haiki cocked his head. "Don't you find it confusing?"

My ears swiveled and I listened intently. The music was twisting through my thoughts. I tried to quiet my mind but there was no escaping the waterfalls with their mesmerizing prisms. If anything, they were growing more lurid as the day drew on.

Haiki was running his tongue over his muzzle. "I think it's foxcraft."

My ears flicked back. "What's foxcraft?"

"The water, the rainbows . . ."

Old forces defend the lands surrounding the Rock.

Is this what Siffrin had meant?

Rapid blinking sapped the power of a slimmer—there were things a fox might do against other crafts. My tail jerked and a murmur escaped my throat. I focused my mind and pushed the sounds away. With an effort, my thoughts grew clearer. The music subsided, leaving only a tinkle of water. The rainbows flickered in and out of view.

My muzzle wrinkled and I watched Haiki thoughtfully. "Do you know, I think you're right . . ." I shook my head. "I feel a bit muddled. It's the waterfalls, isn't it? All the colors."

"And the sounds too," Haiki agreed.

Simmi's ears pointed out at angles. Her whiskers flexed. "It goes," she gasped. "When you focus your mind, it goes. You're right, Haiki, it must be foxcraft! But who's doing it?"

"Perhaps the Elders themselves." I looked warily along the sharp edge of the rocks to the cascades of water. "It feels like a trap."

"We're going around in circles," said Haiki. "I don't think we're any nearer to the Rock."

The nagging returned, feathery like the pale hairs of my ears. Just out of reach.

I'd forgotten something.

Siffrin's voice sprang into my thoughts. *Jana knows about Isla, but she can't know of your skulk. I need to go ahead to assure her that it's safe. I can return for Isla, Simmi, and Tao if she agrees.*

Jana, I realized, *not all the Elders.* Why only Jana?

That thought, just out of reach. I drew in a deep breath and slowed down my heart rate, as though I was about to slimmer. My vision blurred and I closed my eyes.

With a jolt, I remembered what Siffrin had said back in the Snarl when he'd talked of the Elders.

They are all from the Wildlands, from different skulks. They gather only rarely at the Elder Rock, a raised shaft in a circle of trees. It lies between the Darklands and the Upper Wildlands, but few who search will find it.

"The Rock!" I hissed. "The Elders meet there only rarely—the rest of the year, they live secret lives among different skulks. That's why Siffrin spoke about finding *Jana*, not the Elders—because the Elders wouldn't have been at the Rock."

Simmi stared at me. "What are you saying? When will the Elders be there?"

The tingling beat rose through my paws. Suddenly I knew. "Malinta," I breathed. "Malinta and the gloaming— they're the only nights the Elders meet."

Simmi's jaw fell slack as she absorbed what I was saying. "But malinta . . . that's tonight!"

"*Tonight?*" The shadows were already long as our tails; the sun was hovering low. "We have to get off the cliffs!" I peered over the rock edge, trying to see beyond the water. Wondering how we would get away. "Where's Tao?"

Simmi's ears flicked back. "Just behind me . . . or he was." Her fur rose in alarm. "How long has he been gone?" She started quickly along the rocks, her paws slipping on puddles.

"Careful!" I urged, close on her tail.

Simmi hopped down a set of flat rocks, calling her brother's name. "Tao? Tao, are you there?" The rocks rounded the cliff, curving beneath another waterfall. When I reached around the edge of the cliff, I caught sight of Tao's brush. He was very close to a waterfall, extending his forepaw.

"Get away from there!" snapped Simmi. Her back was arched in panic.

Tao's voice was soft. "I'm touching the colors." He allowed the water to tumble onto his fur. At this angle, I could see his paw dangling over the edge of the cliff. He extended his foreleg, a dreamy look on his face.

I padded cautiously behind Simmi. "He's under a spell."

She turned back to me. "We have to do something!"

I knew that with enough focus I could stifle the foxcraft—but how could I convince Tao to do that too? "We need to distract him. Make lots of noise!"

Tao was edging closer to the cliff face. He touched his nose against the waterfall, showering the air with spray. A moment later he pushed his head through the stream so that it disappeared from view.

Simmi was wild-eyed. "What sort of noise?"

I threw back my head and started yelping a distress call. Simmi added her shrill cry to mine and Haiki began barking.

Tao showed no sign of having heard us. Did the waterfall block every sound beyond its deathly whirl?

Simmi squealed and pounced down to her brother. She clamped her fangs around his brush, still shrilling through her teeth. Tao's shoulders jerked and he tugged at his tail. Simmi bit harder.

Tao turned on her angrily. "What are you doing?" he howled over the yelps, but we kept going, our voices sharp on the air.

Simmi shook his tail as though it was prey.

"Stop that!" he squealed, trying to push his sister away.

"Who are you?" I cried. "Who *are* you?"

Tao shook his head in confusion. "I'm . . ." His jaw fell slack.

Simmi chomped down on his tail again.

"Ow!" he pulled against her ineffectually.

"Who are you?"

"I'm Tao from the Upper Wildlands!"

"Are you sure?"

"I'm sure!"

I let out a long breath. Haiki stopped barking and Simmi released her brother's tail. He pulled it to him, licking the wound she had left. "You could have broken it," he whimpered.

"I should have." Simmi's face was twisted into a snarl. "Why did you wander off like that? Didn't you hear what Isla said? We need to reach the Rock by malinta!"

Tao looked across the edge of the cliff. "I didn't mean to."

"This place is cursed," I said. "You didn't know what you were doing."

Tao frowned. "The sounds . . . the colors."

The tremble of malinta touched my paw pads. We had to find a way out of this beautiful maze. I wondered what Siffrin would do.

Why hadn't he returned to the den?

My gaze whipped over the edge of the cliffs. I noticed a

narrow ascent through two boulders. "This way," I urged. I started climbing a series of rutted rocks, leading the others uphill. But as we reached the top, the path closed before us in a kaleidoscope of waterfalls. Beyond their rainbow colors I saw flashes of sky where the rocks fell away. The light was waning but the colors still danced in the spray.

There was no way out.

Haiki spoke uncertainly. "We'll have to go back . . . to go around."

"Go around *what*?" snapped Simmi, her patience fraying. "Haven't you heard what Isla said? This is a trap. Someone doesn't want us to reach the Elder Rock—maybe the Elders themselves. If we go back we'll just be treading circles. We'll never make it for malinta. How long will Tao resist the call of the waterfalls?"

"I'm trying," he whimpered, his voice thick with shame. "But it's strong." He ran his tongue over his muzzle. "I just want to touch the colors. If only I could touch them very quickly."

"Do you want me to bite you again?" Simmi hissed.

Haiki's voice rose sharply. "What are we going to do? If we miss malinta, the Elders won't be there. This whole trip will have been for nothing . . . We have to get there for malinta!"

I was hardly listening. Squinting through the spray, I caught a glimpse of the sunset. Light was gliding through

214

the sky like a leaping fox trailing a crimson brush. With a start I remembered what Siffrin had told me.

The journey to the Elder Rock is hazardous. There is the deathway, woodlands, and a path that appears with the last brush of dusk . . . Not all who search will find what they are looking for.

As the sun began to sink from view, the orange foxtail deepened. The fox's body stretched over the sky and its pale tip brushed the waterfalls. For an instant, it lit a passage through the water, a tunnel that flickered before my eyes. Then the fox's tail descended and darkness came.

19

"Quickly, follow me!" I started toward the waterfall that had revealed the passage.

"Not you as well!" yelped Simmi, shoving in front of me. "I thought you were stronger than that."

Haiki was quick to jump in. "Don't be fooled, Isla! You'll fall to your death!"

My ears flicked back. "There's a path over the rocks. We need to go quickly, before we lose it—don't stand in my way."

The whispering song of the water grew louder, crowding around me, confusing my thoughts. The memory of the passage was fading. If I lost my nerve now, I would start to doubt what I'd seen. I shoved past Simmi, ducking beneath the waterfall before the others could stop me.

Cold water splashed against my muzzle. Its tinkling song rose sharply, bursting into a frenzied thrumming, screaming in my ears. I felt a bite of wind and in that wet, blind instant I feared I'd made a mistake.

Was I stepping over a cliff edge?

But my wavering forepaw smacked down on solid stone. The thrum of the water subsided in a hush of spray. Blinking away the droplets from my eyes, I saw that I was perched on a narrow shelf of rock that plunged down in a spiral. I spotted no waterfalls along its dark route, just a dizzying route downhill.

I turned toward the waterfall. "I'm all right!" My voice echoed back to me.

I was reluctant to approach the water, recalling the screeching thrum that had risen in my ears. Instead of nosing toward it, I pierced the spray with a forepaw. "Can you hear me?" I barked. "There's a path here."

As I withdrew, Simmi's snout stabbed through the water. "Are you sure it's all right?"

"Yes, steep but safe," I answered.

She drew back. I heard her barking instructions at Tao over the fizz of the waterfall. A moment later, he rushed through the spray to stand by my side. Simmi followed, with a terrified Haiki close behind her. As the gray fox shivered on the gloomy stone shelf, I wondered at how he had risked so much to distract the Taken. He was not a fox of natural courage, and yet he'd protected us.

More than Siffrin has, I thought bitterly. *Why am I surprised? Of course he was going to let us down.*

Unless . . . What if something happened to him?

There wasn't time to think about that now. The moon grazed the tops of the distant hills. The lurching path was growing darker as light faded along the edges of the world. We had to hurry.

I led the way down as quickly as I dared, the others silent on my tail. My head felt clearer than it had since we'd left the forest. The strange enchantment of the rocks was drifting away. In its place, a rhythm rose through the earth, stronger now. The call of malinta.

The air was moist, mizzling with rain. Canista's Lights glanced between the clouds. I moved quickly—too quickly for the damp ground. For a moment, I lost my footing, and my paw skimmed the lip of the stone. I drew in my breath and slowed my pace.

Soon, the path before me was close to black. Only a thread of silver light hinted at the steep descent.

Eventually I felt the land level out beneath my paws. The path vanished in a crumble of pebbles. The smell of cedar filled my nose. As the last whisker of light fell beyond the horizon, I took my first cautious steps into an ancient forest. Giant branches reached overhead, hanging off trunks as thick as furless dens. The breath of the trees enclosed us.

"This is the Elder Wood. This is where we'll find the blood-bark tree." I couldn't explain my certainty, but it swelled inside me—the Rock was close.

Tao was sniffing, his muzzle pressed against the soil.

Simmi's voice was wary. "It's *so* dark. I've never known a night like this."

Haiki padded alongside me. "We can't go now, not without light. We'll have to wait till dawn."

The hum of the earth was stronger on the mossy ground. I blinked through the darkness. The vibration that touched my paw pads was growing more intense. Quivers rose through my legs and along my tail.

"We can't wait, malinta's here." I started bounding, my paws scarcely grazing the soft ground. "Quickly!" I barked, "We're out of time!"

"We'll bang into tree trunks," Tao muttered, though he started to follow.

"How do you know the way?" Simmi called.

"Look over there!" An amber light was blossoming over the Elder Wood, rising far in the distance. I could feel my paws tugging toward it with each thump of the earth. *It's the Rock*, I thought. *The Elders are there!*

I swung around, intending to say this, and stopped in my tracks. Haiki had fallen behind. He was frozen to the spot, gazing over the trees.

"What's wrong?"

I saw him in silhouette. His ears were flat. "Maybe I'll wait for you here."

"This was your idea!" I gave Haiki a hard look.

He shifted from paw to paw. "It's like you said, the Elders won't help us. It just took me a while to realize that." His voice trembled and his tail was stiff.

I couldn't understand the change in him. "Has something happened?" I blinked into the shadows between the ancient trees.

Simmi's hackles rose. "Haiki, are you crazy? After we've come so far?" She turned to scurry into the wood.

"Come on!" Tao growled over his shoulder.

I paused, cocking my head at Haiki. His whiskers trembled and he dipped his muzzle.

"Tell me what's wrong," I said softly.

The gray fox looked up. Our eyes met. "Isla, I . . ." A bat screeched overhead. Haiki shook his fur. "It's nothing." He hurried past me, following Simmi and Tao into the wood.

The pungent smell of blossoms filled the air and the ground thumped against our paws. Amber foxtails billowed against a dark sky. I hurried as quickly as I dared through brush and ferns, feeling the soft slap of greenery against my face. Edging around a tree trunk I lost my footing, tripping over a knotted root. I gave a small yelp as I tumbled, rolling back onto my paws.

"Are you all right?" asked Tao, close behind me.

I shook my paw. It throbbed where I'd struck it against the root but I was able to put my weight on it. "Yes, fine."

Malinta thrummed. I felt its power radiating from the soil. The air felt charged, like before a storm. Canista's Lights glanced between the clouds. They pulsed white against the velvet sky, illuminating the ancient wood.

The light was further away than it seemed. We ran through the night but it scarcely seemed to grow closer.

Bushes and leaves leaped into my path and I dodged them, panting hard. What if we missed malinta? If the Elders vanished, where would we go? I couldn't think that way, not now. We would find the Rock. The Elders would help us.

I pictured Pirie.

They have to.

I risked a glance into the sky and my breath snagged in my throat. The moon was bleeding into black, disappearing beyond the horizon.

Moonset.

The most dangerous time of night, when red-eyed foxes stalked the Wildlands.

But not here. Not close to the Elders.

The amber foxtails looped overhead. We weren't far now. We'd make it. I slowed my pace, looking back to the others. Simmi and Tao scrambled to a halt, panting alongside me. Haiki stood a few paces behind, his tail drifting low.

The light gave a strange tinge to the giant trees. Most had the same dusty hue to their leathery trunks, with upturned branches and small unfurling buds. They hunched toward one another, as though conspiring.

But one tree was different.

Its gnarly trunk was the deep red of dried blood. Its branches were so stooped that they skimmed the floor of the wood, so twisted they resembled angry beasts. Its tiny buds were small red tears.

Around the great curving trunk of the blood-bark tree were more of the jagged, light-flecked stones, like the ones on the cliffs. A beam of amber pointed down from the sky. The stones sparkled beneath its touch, edging around a huge rock circle with a large, flat mount.

My whiskers prickled. *The Elder Rock.* A swath of amber fog coiled around the shimmering stones. The figures on the Rock were blurred silhouettes.

Haiki hung back, eyes wide with fear.

Simmi and Tao exchanged worried glances.

"What now?" Simmi whispered.

For a moment I floundered. Was it safe to approach the Elders like this?

The beat of malinta thumped against my paws, jolting me from these thoughts.

Have you come all this way just to run and hide?

I took a step forward. The amber light grew brighter, though the shapes on the rock remained fuzzy. I counted five . . . six . . . Had one of the missing Elders returned?

"Jana?" I called but my voice was faint beneath the drumming earth. I stalked forward a few paces. The amber fog floated in front of me. I reached out a forepaw—

A shot of fire spread through my chest and I tumbled, blinded by colors. Heat exploded from my skin. Every hair on my body shrieked. I was spinning in the kaleidoscope, into the bleeding center of the world.

With a jerk of my legs I was back in the wood, lying on a patch of moss. For a moment I struggled to breathe, as though someone had thumped me in the gut. I blinked to see Simmi looming above me. Tao and Haiki came into view.

"What happened?" hissed Simmi. "Are you all right?"

I drew in a slow breath. The pain had gone almost instantly. I rose, shaking off my fur. "The shana."

We stood watching the amber light.

I cleared my throat. "Elders, please let us pass," I said gravely. "We want to speak with you."

Malinta beat against my paws. The wind rose in the branches of the ancient trees. My ears twisted forward and back.

Isla.

The voice seemed to drift in the air, as if the fog had spoken.

My heart leaped. "Yes."

We have been waiting for you. The voice paused. *There are others.*

I felt Simmi tense by my side. I swallowed down the fear

in my throat and spoke into the swirling fog. "They're with me. Simmi, Tao, and Haiki from the Wildlands. We need your help. The Mage—"

Do not speak of him beyond the Rock.

I clamped my jaws shut. Against the beat of the earth, there was silence. We stood some time as the fur spiked along my back. Then the fog began to melt into the darkness of the night.

Five foxes stood in the unfurling mist, their eyes trained on us. I recognized the vixen in the center as Jana, with her slender gray limbs and short tail. I had seen her in maasharm, in Siffrin's memory.

The other four were also elderly foxes. A tall brown male squinted at me, his whiskers spiraling out of his muzzle in odd directions. Next to him was a ginger-and-white vixen who scarcely reached his shoulders. The vixen's ears were huge, too large for her small head. They sprang out at angles. She lowered her snout and sniffed, then cocked her head curiously, as though she'd smelled something strange. By her side, an auburn vixen glared at us.

The last Elder Fox was a male with fur the color of sand. His muzzle was gray, speckled with black. I noticed that one of his fangs was missing.

I felt the heat of their appraising gazes. I took in the outlines of their tatty pelts. I might have passed them in the wood and never realized their power.

But their eyes shone brilliantly, wide and bright as the moon.

We are the Elders of the Rock.

They spoke together with one voice. I stared at them, dumbstruck. Beyond the old foxes, wisps of amber mist still floated, distorting my view of the Rock.

Why have you come?

I cleared my throat. "My brother's missing. It could have something to do with—" I paused. *Do not speak of him beyond the Rock.* "With *him*. I seek your help. I need to know the secret of wa'akkir. And—" I looked around for Simmi.

She stepped next to me. "Our skulk was attacked. We have no home. We cannot fight pleached foxes."

"We need foxcraft," said Tao. "Like Isla, we want to learn wa'akkir."

The auburn vixen stared down her muzzle at us. "Wa'akkir is not for every fox."

I fought the urge to shrink from her hard stare. "But it *should* be. Skulks are being attacked and they can't fight back."

Jana's ears rotated. "Siffrin told us you would come. You may enter the dominion of the Rock. We can talk more once we raise the shana." Her eyes trailed over us searchingly. "Enemies may be close."

My whiskers tingled. "Siffrin's here?"

I saw him then through the fading mist. He trotted across the Rock, his red coat gleaming in the starlight.

My forepaw wavered above the flat expanse of rock. My voice was tiny. "You didn't come back."

Siffrin's eyes were huge, the centers black discs against golden light. "I tried," he said. "When I reached the pines, the Taken were waiting—it was like they were expecting me. I had no choice, I had to run. One of the Narral was with them, a fox called Koch."

My whiskers trembled. I didn't know what to think.

Siffrin appealed to me with his eyes. "I couldn't risk leading them to the Elders, you must understand that. I ran east into unknown valleys and north along the Raging River. I didn't return for a couple of nights. I had to be sure that I'd thrown them off my scent. After the coyotes . . ." He shook his head, his ears flat. "I knew that you might not understand. But if Koch or the Taken made it to the Rock . . ." A flicker of fear darkened Siffrin's face. He seemed to remember the others, tilting his head toward Simmi and Tao. "You got here without me. Your ma and fa will be proud."

"They're gone," whined Tao. "They've been pleached."

Simmi's voice quavered. "The rest of the skulk were murdered. Even Greatfa. Even Mox."

Siffrin gasped, his tail leaping straight behind him. "I had no idea."

My throat was dry. "Koch . . . is he stocky, with short legs and a greasy coat? He was with the Taken when they attacked the den." For an instant I thought of Mox, curled like a cub, but not in sleep.

The Elders stiffened.

Siffrin's eyes darted to mine. "Koch shouldn't have found the skulk—I led those foxes away!"

Jana's gray ears twitched. "I don't like what I'm hearing. Always, our enemies are one step ahead of us."

The ginger-and-white vixen raised her muzzle. Her nostrils pulsed. "I sense a shape-shifter," she said ominously. "One without foxcraft."

The fur was rigid at the back of my neck. How could you shape-shift without wa'akkir?

Jana glared beyond us, into the dark wood. "We need to weave the shana. Without it we're exposed."

I hesitated, staring at Siffrin.

He stared back. "Don't you believe me?"

I wasn't sure. My head was muddled.

"Step onto the Rock," urged Jana.

I climbed the jagged stones, careful to avoid their sharp edges, stepping over them onto the smooth Rock. The beat of malinta jolted my limbs. It was stronger now, almost unbearable. Simmi and Tao sprang next to me, casting wary looks at Siffrin.

The male with the curling whiskers peered beyond me. "What about you?"

Haiki was standing alone on the grass. His lips twitched but no sound emerged.

"Come on," I called. "They need to protect the Rock."

I followed his lips as they formed a word.

"Sorry."

I cocked my head. "Sorry for what?"

His eyes slid toward me. His voice scarcely rose over the beat of the earth. "He took my skulk. I had no choice. He made me track you in the Graylands and wait in the gorge until you came."

A chill crept through me. "What do you mean?"

"I needed to get you to the Elders, but Siffrin saw too much . . . He had to be stopped. That's why I brought the coyotes."

I heard Siffrin yelp in surprise. Haiki's gaze shot over my shoulder to where the red-furred fox was standing. Then he looked beyond us, into the dark expanses of the wood.

The tips of my paws were numb. I couldn't feel my tail. What was he saying? It didn't make sense. *No*, I thought. *No, no, no . . .* I stumbled, unsteady.

Haiki's eyes were full of sorrow. "It was always about the Elders. They wanted you, Isla. They'd let you pass. I couldn't do it alone." He lowered his muzzle, his voice a desperate whine. "I never imagined how hard it would be . . . how much I'd care about you, Isla. I'm sick with guilt, torn on the inside. Please understand. I'm not a bad fox. I'm just like you—I'd do *anything* to get my family back. He said he'd free my skulk if I led them here."

A shape-shifter. One without foxcraft.

Suddenly it was hard to breathe. "Led who?"

Behind me, Jana yowled in alarm. "The shana!"

That moment I saw them surge out of the darkness. The red-eyed foxes burst past Haiki to race across the grass. Siffrin sprang in front of me but two large foxes crashed against him, flinging him onto the glittering stones. In an instant, the Taken surrounded us.

Still they kept coming, racing between the trees in an endless torrent. Their backs were arched, their hackles up, their pointed teeth exposed.

The shana was broken.

The Elders surrounded.

The Taken were on the Rock.

20

The auburn-furred vixen started chanting.

"Come together, rays of light; comfort me in deadly night . . ."

One of the Taken pounced on her and sank his teeth into her flank. The Elder spluttered, unable to chant. The Rock exploded into chaos. A tawny fox leaped at Tao, bringing him down. The tall brown Elder slimmered, disappearing from view. He reappeared an instant later with his jaws pressed at the fox's throat.

The auburn vixen rose to her paws. The tip of her tail started glowing as she murmured beneath her breath.

"Don't let her chant!" snarled one of the Taken, his eyes pulsing red.

The Mage is speaking through him.

The pleached foxes turned on the auburn vixen. They snapped at her tail and pulled her down. She was lost in a scrum of claws and teeth.

All around me, foxes were fighting, hissing and spitting, slamming into one another. The small ginger-and-white vixen threw an attacker off the Rock and grabbed another by his throat. I could hardly believe she had the strength in her short, skinny legs.

Tao karakked like a raven, scaring one of the foxes away.

But the Taken kept coming, a swell of red-eyed foxes bursting out from the trees.

The earth beat louder.

Ka-thump! Ka-thump!

Jana bounded past the Taken and leaped into the air, her lips fluttering rapidly. For an instant she froze, a blur of ginger and jags of gold. A terrifying howl tore over the Rock. She landed in the shape of a great coyote, muzzle wrinkled with rage. Several foxes recoiled in terror, beginning to flee.

"It's a trick!" cried the fox with the pulsing red eyes. "Don't you dare run away!"

Jana flashed her coyote fangs. She spun in the air, a whirl of blues and grays, shifting into a savage dog. Red-eyed foxes tumbled off the flat mount, thumping onto the sharp stones. Still more kept coming, scurrying over the stones and slipping over the Rock.

The Elders were wildly outnumbered. Four or five foxes set upon Jana, crunching down on her legs.

The Elder Rock shuddered.

"Isla, look out!" Siffrin was fighting his way back onto the Rock, shoving a pleached fox aside. Two others lunged at me, their white fangs bared.

With a murmur I slimmered, twisting out of their reach. Simmi was tussling with a tan fox by my side. They smacked into my flank, breaking my slimmer, and I backed away, exposed.

A mottled-furred fox wheeled around to face me. His yellow eyes flashed in the starlight. I could smell the acid pall of his coat as he launched toward me. He threw open his jaws. His breath was cinders.

My blood pulsed fire through my limbs. My lips peeled back but no sound escaped my throat. My gaze shot to Siffrin but he was surrounded, blocked by four or five Taken.

The night was pierced by a flash of lightning. White heat struck the Rock, and malinta thundered. The wind rose wildly through the trees and the foxes stumbled, as though the ground had grown uneven. My attackers tumbled away from me, unable to keep their balance. I clung to the slippery stone as best I could. What was happening? Was it malinta? Was it a sudden storm?

The screeching wind dropped abruptly. Through the scramble of foxes, I spotted one Elder standing boldly at the center of the Rock—the sandy-furred male was panting but his gaze was steady.

Jana threw back her head. "Elders, regroup!"

Another Elder, the tall brown male, tried to fight his way to her. The auburn vixen was shaking off one of the Taken, blood running down her white chest. Whenever an Elder began to slimmer, or to utter the chant for wa'akkir, foxes converged on them, shattering the spell. I spun around, breathless. Haiki had vanished and the Taken were still rushing from the wood. There was nowhere left to run.

Jana pressed closer to Siffrin. Between flashes of battling foxes, I saw her whisper in his ear.

"Foxling!" snarled one of the Taken, a vixen with a long brown muzzle. "The time of the Elders is over! You cannot succeed against the Mage." She rolled on her haunches, preparing to pounce.

"Stop!" I yowled. "The Mage stole your will. He's *making* you do this."

The fox scowled, her red eyes gleaming. Saliva bubbled at her jaws. "I serve the Master."

"He doesn't *own* you!" My ears flicked forward in appeal. "You were more than this once. You were a free fox. You had a family, a skulk. Don't you remember?"

Doubt crossed her eyes. Her foreleg twitched, the mark of the broken rose bruise-black in the low light. Then her gaze became vague and her body grew rigid. "I have no family." She sprang and I scrabbled away from her, stumbling against another pleached fox. He spat and I karakked, mimicking the furious bark of a dog. The fox flinched and I darted across the Rock, dodging the others in my path.

A thump across my back brought me down.

Foul breath drifted close to my ear. "I have you, foxling. You won't escape."

I caught a glimpse of the fox's jaws, the spit that bubbled at the corner of his mouth. I bucked against him but he pinned me down harder.

"Leave her alone!" shrieked Tao. He crunched on the fox's tail. Simmi dived to his side, snapping her jaws around the fox's paw. With a screech, the fox released me.

My heart crashed over malinta's beat.

A line of three Taken leaped into my path and I braced myself, too panicked to run. But before they reached me, they changed direction, breaking for the edge of the Rock with shrill yelps. A great black dog drove between them. She dropped to my side as I cowered in terror.

"Isla, are you all right?" It was Siffrin's voice. He'd appeared as the fearsome dog from the Snarl. "We need you," he gasped. "Shaya's injured."

I blinked at him. "I don't understand."

His eyes were wide. "We need your maa for shana-sharm."

From the edge of my vision, I saw Tao back into two Taken foxes. Simmi was fighting her way toward him but other foxes blocked her path.

"Trust me, Isla," Siffrin urged.

Trust no one but family, for a fox has no friends.

Siffrin's eyes were golden against the dog's savage face.

Fear fluttered at my ears like moths. "Show me what to do."

"Follow me!" He bounded across the Rock, shunting foxes out of his path. He reached Simmi and murmured in her ear. She spun around immediately, dodging the Taken. In flashes I saw her fight through the frenzy to Tao. The two of them battled to the edge of the shimmering stones.

It was a struggle to keep up with Siffrin. I slimmered again, down on my belly, shuffling past red-eyed Taken. I didn't get far before a fox trod on my paw. The slimmer broken, I scampered as fast as I could. I had almost reached Siffrin at the edge of the Rock when a sharp pain shot through my tail.

"Not so fast, foxling!"

The vixen's eyes were caked in yellow gunk. Scarlet veins ran through their dark centers. A shadow crossed them, another fox. For a beat, I saw him clearly—his acid eyes, his pointed ears, and the tail that swished from side to side. A tail that ended in a stump.

Ice ran through my blood.

"It's the Mage!" I yelped at the red-eyed fox. "He's making you do this. You're pleached, don't you see?"

The fox seemed surprised. She blinked and the Mage disappeared from her eyes. I broke free, diving over another attacker to land at Siffrin's side.

He spoke as though I'd always been there. "I need you to chant with us. When Jana says the word, jump off the Rock."

"But they're so many," I whined. "What good will it—"

"There isn't time! Repeat the chant: 'Come together, rays of light; comfort me in deadly night. Weave a wall of thickest mist; every fiend and foe resist.' Whatever happens, don't stop chanting. Get ready to jump off the Rock."

I did as he told me, mumbling the words. "Come together, rays of light . . ." A fox pounced at me but Siffrin lunged at him, still in the shape of the dog. Another charged toward us. Siffrin threw his great forepaws at the fox, sending him toppling over other attackers.

Come together, rays of light; comfort me in deadly night.

Despite the snarls and barks from the Rock, and the furious beat of malinta, the Elders' voices reached me like an echo in my ear, so I heard the chant in harmony. The crashing thump of my heart slowed down. I still saw the turmoil on the Rock—the fighting, the bloodshed—but it floated past my thoughts.

Weave a wall of thickest mist; every fiend and foe resist.

My thoughts were amber. Was it I who threw wisps of color around the Rock? They drifted past the fighting foxes. Curls of mist trailed the light. Slowly it thickened, smudging my vision. Through tendrils of amber, the Taken paused. They blinked and turned in confusion.

Jana's voice rang in my ears, as though she spoke directly to my thoughts. *Jump!*

I gazed into the amber light. The fog was so thick that I could barely see my own forelegs. Malinta thrummed against my paws, soothing, numbing. A deep calm took hold of me. My lips still tripped over the chant, but I hardly recognized the words.

Come together, rays of light.

A powerful thump struck my flank and I tumbled. For an instant, I was in free fall, plummeting through nothingness. Then I landed on the mossy ground, just shy of the jagged stones. I yelped and scrambled to my paws. I was standing before the Rock in the circle of trees. The wood around us was sharp and clear—the fog stayed wrapped over the flat mount.

Only the Taken remained on the Rock. Dotted along the outskirts of the stones were the Elders. Simmi and Tao crouched by the blood-bark tree. Siffrin was by my side, no longer shifted into a dog but back in his own form.

"You struck me!" I gasped. "I could have hit the stones."

He was unrepentant. "I had to get you off the Rock. Keep chanting!"

I drew in my breath. "Come together, rays of light; comfort me in deadly night."

The voices of the Elders danced in my ears. Against the sweet, shrill harmony, I caught another sound. The foxes on the Rock had started barking.

"What's going on?" one snarled.

"Just another pathetic trick. Forget their foxcraft and illusion. The Elders won't escape. There's nowhere to run!"

Still I kept chanting.

The amber light deepened. The mist thickened into a cloying fog. The air was sickly. I could no longer see the foxes on the Rock, though I sensed the tang of their putrid fur.

Jana stood a few paces from me at the base of a mossy tree. I saw her turn up her muzzle. Her eyes glowed white with a shimmer of green.

Malinta quivered beneath my paws. The tip of Jana's tail burned silver. I looked around. The other Elders' tail-tips were glowing too.

Something was happening.

The fog was gathering over the Rock. The amber light swept in circles, deepening to orange.

The yelps of the Taken grew louder. Some fought to escape, pushing past one another to the edge of the Rock. Those who touched the shana fell back with screams of pain.

There was choking and gasping, a blur of writhing bodies. A desperate whine broke through: "No air! Can't breathe!"

Vague silhouettes flailed beyond the wall of fog. It sank lower, the light turning orange. The words of the chant dissolved on my tongue.

"Keep going," warned Siffrin. "If they escape, we're dead."

The dreaminess had left me. I didn't stop chanting, but my limbs were cold. Once those were foxes just like us. They didn't have a choice . . .

Come together, rays of light; comfort me in deadly night.

The yelps of terror faded. Even the beat of malinta seemed to still. All I could hear was the chant rising over the wood.

Weave a wall of thickest mist; every fiend and foe resist.

The fog had grown so dense and dark that the silhouettes vanished in its sticky embrace. It wrapped around the Elder Rock, a constricting pelt of crimson. There was a fizzling sound as the fog sank. For an instant, I saw paw prints etched in the stone, the echo of the Taken. Then the fog dispersed, the red light died, and the paw prints disappeared.

21

Dawn broke over the Elder Rock. At the edge of the Rock, beneath the overhanging branches of the blood-bark tree, Simmi and Tao were curled together in sleep. At the center, where shadows didn't reach, light blazed against the stones. The shana swirled around us, dancing along the outskirts of the Rock, protecting us from harm.

The beat of the earth had stilled. In its wake, the wood was renewed. I heard the chirrup of songbirds from beyond the shana. The scent of blossoms was thick in the air.

Four of the Elders padded toward me. The tan fox followed more slowly, limping. One of his forepaws twisted at an angle. I doubted he could run very fast. How did he cope in the wild?

Siffrin hung back. His brush swept the stone and he

yawned indifferently, but I caught him watching from the corner of my eye.

"As you know, I am Jana," the gray fox said. "This is Mika." She nodded at the tiny ginger-and-white vixen. "She is mistress of pashanda. In a trance, Mika calls to the winds and they answer."

The small vixen dropped her muzzle. "I should have sensed the Taken. I knew something wasn't right, but they've been banished from this wood so long I thought they lacked the nerve to come." Her voice was high, like a cub's, but I could tell from her whiskery face that she was old. Her long claws tapped the stone. "It was a foolish mistake and I'm sorry for it."

My tail crept to my flank. A deep ache throbbed in my chest. It was *my* fault, not hers. I'd brought Haiki, and he'd led the Taken.

The small vixen sniffed; her ears twisted back. She angled her snout from side to side, as though she was drinking me in from my scent. Her yellow eyes seemed to look through me.

"Siffrin was right," she murmured. "The cub's maa is strong."

"Yes," agreed Jana. She glanced at the tall brown-furred male with the curling whiskers. "This is Brin. He is an expert at slimmering. He can cross the wood without being seen."

"You exaggerate, Jana," drawled the tall brown male. "I do draw breath sometimes. You make it sound like I'm half-dead already." For a flicker he disappeared from view, reappearing so quickly that I wasn't sure if he'd really slimmered. The set of his jaw was firm but his small eyes sparkled.

"And this is Shaya." Jana tipped her muzzle to the stern auburn vixen. "She has a gift for drawing on maa. Maa-sharm, shana-sharm—we couldn't do without her."

Shaya gave a haughty flick of her tail. Looking at this cool-eyed vixen, I couldn't imagine maa-sharm with her. I noticed the scars along her flank and a clot of blood at the base of her neck. I remembered how she'd tried to chant but the Taken hadn't let her—they'd known to target her. The Mage must have told them.

Jana turned to the other male. "Kolo is master of karakking."

I tore my gaze away from Shaya. Karakking was hardly a higher art. I could do it back in the Snarl, before I'd even heard of foxcraft.

Kolo must have guessed what I was thinking. His muzzle tightened and his ears rolled back. He threw open his gray jaws. His missing fang made him look roguish. Suddenly the trees started groaning, their branches shaking violently. I cringed against the whirr of wind through shrieking leaves. A clap of lightning tore through the trees, and the rumble of thunder rose over the wood.

I leaped into the air, my fur on end.

The fox's lips closed over his teeth, and the ancient trees grew still.

I gasped in amazement. I remembered the lightning and wind that had struck the Rock. Was this really a form of karakking? It was more urgent and powerful than any I'd imagined.

Siffrin was still watching from a distance.

I drew down my puffed-up tail. "I didn't come for tricks."

Jana's whiskers flexed. "I see you have a temper, young fox. We know why you came. And you brought *others*." She cast her gaze over the Rock. Simmi and Tao had woken at Kolo's karakking—but I guessed Jana meant someone else. My tail drooped guiltily.

I lowered my muzzle. "Haiki used me. I led the Taken to the Rock." I couldn't meet Jana's eye.

"All this time, we feared the Mage would capture you for your maa. But he was cleverer than us. He let you live. He must have known you'd come here and that we'd let you pass."

"He manipulated the gray, just to be sure," said the yellow-eyed Mika. "The young fox wasn't lying when he spoke of his skulk. He's desperate to find them—hunger and loneliness burned from every hair of his pelt."

No one had seen Haiki since malinta. My claws flexed when I thought of him. I gathered the ache in my chest and

243

channeled it into rage—it was easier to bear. One day I'd find that traitor, and I'd have my revenge. I would never forgive him, not after what he'd done.

"At least Koch didn't come," said Jana. "The Mage doesn't want to risk the death of another Narral, especially after Karka."

Mika frowned. "I sense Koch. There are others. They are stalking the edges of the wood."

I looked up. The amber shana glided around the Rock, protecting us from harm.

Brin blinked at me kindly. "We should have been seven . . . Then Shaya was injured. With only four Elders left to chant, we couldn't have woven the shana. It is thanks to you that we trapped the Taken."

My shoulders sank. "They couldn't breathe."

Kolo ran his tongue over his gray muzzle. "They were the Mage's skulk. They would have killed us in an instant."

"They didn't know what they were doing." I could hardly bear to think about the Taken on the Rock. My gaze drifted to Siffrin, who was washing his fur. The mark of the broken rose was etched on his foreleg, beneath his glossy coat. "It can be reversed, can't it? The pleaching?"

"What does she know about pleaching?" muttered Shaya.

Jana spoke more gently. "It was for Siffrin," she confirmed. From the corner of my eye, I saw the red-furred fox start. "That was before. Things have changed. The Mage has expanded his dark arts and he holds the Taken close. We cannot unearth the harm he's caused . . ." Her gray tail sank with regret.

My whiskers twitched. "But it isn't impossible?"

Simmi and Tao were stalking closer with nervous steps. They must have been thinking of Flint and Karo.

Jana's eyes were as gray as her fur. "These are treacherous times. The Mage is more powerful than ever, while we are weaker." She tilted her muzzle toward Simmi and Tao. "You probably know him as the Tailless Seer."

Simmi's hackles flicked up and Tao whimpered.

Jana turned back to me. "Siffrin told you that we're missing two Elders. Keeveny was our expert in pleaching, and now he is gone."

"Is he the Black Fox?" I asked.

I saw Brin and Mika stiffen. Kolo drew in his breath, and Shaya's tail flew straight behind her.

Jana was grave. "Métis is the Black Fox. Exceptional at foxcraft, he's master of all arts, from slimmering to maasharm. But rash, impatient, and with a scarlet temper." She shared a lingering glance with Shaya and cleared her throat. "We have long guessed that the Mage is an Elder. We hope it is not him."

I shuddered at the thought. A fox who could karak like Kolo, who could slimmer like Brin . . . A fox with Mika's talent for reading the wind would have formidable power.

Kolo tilted his gray muzzle. "Keeveny and Métis were rivals from neighboring skulks. Keeveny may not be the Black Fox, but ambition is its own dark art. If he is the Mage, he should not be underestimated."

Jana dipped her head in acknowledgment. "There is a bitterness in Keeveny, an acid to his tongue."

Neither Elder sounded especially nice. "Is one tailless?"

"No," said Kolo slowly. "Or they weren't when we last saw them."

"At least you have foxcraft," said Simmi in a small voice. "Wildlands foxes are under attack."

Kolo scowled. "You think we aren't aware of that?"

"The Ghost Valley is growing," whined Tao. "Soon our meadow won't exist anymore."

Brin's dark eyes were full of sadness. "It is a tragedy."

Shaya's muzzle tensed. "All the lands surrounding the Darklands are expanding. It is more than a tragedy—it is part of its plan."

Jana shot her a sharp look and my ears pricked up.

"The Mage has a plan?" She'd called him "it." What did that mean?

Jana turned back to me. "His thirst for maa, his army of pleached foxes . . . He needs all the strength he can gather."

It struck me that I'd never really considered this before. *Why* is *the Mage pleaching Wildlands foxes? Why is he growing his lands?*

What does he want?

Jana's tail-tip pulsed silver. She sighed and lowered herself onto her belly. By silent agreement, the other Elders sat too. From a distance, Siffrin cocked his head. He was still pretending not to listen, washing his long tail.

Jana looked from me to Simmi and Tao. "Gather closer, young foxes, let me tell you a story."

We did as she asked, sitting before the Elders with our brushes wrapped around us.

Jana cleared her throat. "Some of Canista's cubs believe in much that cannot be seen with the eyes. The wolves bow to warrior spirits while coyotes glean meaning in the earth and sky."

I remembered the death of the coyote chief.

A blood sun is risen!

Jana went on. "Dogs tell other stories, about the dark times before the furless, when they roamed the Wildlands in packs. They speak of bloody family feuds and a terrible famine that almost led to the end of their kind. The furless were their saviors."

I listened, baffled. How could this be? The furless were violent, cruel . . . I thought of the fluffy white dog from the Snarl. He had seemed quite content. Though it hardly made sense, perhaps the furless were kinder to dogs than they were to foxes.

Jana looked at us sideways. "You're probably thinking,

what about us?" She stretched out her forepaws. "Foxes were always different from wolves and dogs, from the superstitious coyote. For us, it was never about rules. A skulk is not a Bishar—we have no servants, no kings. Above all, we treasure freedom—we do not bow to anyone."

I dipped my head in acknowledgment, recalling what Siffrin had said in the Snarl.

"Perhaps Simmi and Tao know some of the Black Fox fables? They are still popular in the Wildlands."

"He always outwits the furless," said Tao.

"Quite." Jana clenched and relaxed her forepaw in a rhythmic motion. "But we do not have tales of warrior kings, traitors, invaders, or guiding spirits. We leave those to the other sons and daughters of Canista. Except . . ." Her eyes roved over us. "For one. It used to be told to cubs so they learned to value freedom. Most forgot it long ago . . . Only the Elders remember the legend of the White Fox."

A murmur of static rose from the Elders. The amber light of the shana deepened. Siffrin was watching openly now, his long brush flicking back and forth.

"Is the White Fox the same as the Black Fox?" I asked.

Jana let out a long breath. "No," she said at last. "It isn't really a fox at all, not even a cub of Canista. It is not alive—not in the sense that matters."

I glanced at Siffrin, wondering how much of this he already knew. He met my gaze and I snapped my eyes away.

"I don't understand," said Simmi.

It was Mika who explained. "In the early ages of our world, there were other beings. Not living things, exactly, but drifting clots of maa and the dust that skims the stars. They knotted about Canista's Lights like storm clouds. Most faded before they reached the trees and grasses below. They didn't come to anything."

Little Mika shook her head. "The White Fox was a tangle of this strange matter. It broke free from the air, we do not know why. It found its way to our own land. Long ago— before the age of the furless—it sensed the fox running free in the Wildlands. It craved the feeling of wind and rain, the knowledge that it was alive. But it smelled foul to others, like acid and dust."

The fur rippled along my back. *Acid and dust.* The smell of the Taken.

Mika's ears rotated as she spoke. "It settled in the Deep Forest, hidden from prying eyes. There, it fed on the earth's maa, leaching it from the soil. A poisonous yellow murk spread through the forest. It sucked the life from living things, from birds and flowers to butterflies and blades of grass. The Deep Forest rotted."

Mika drew in her forepaws, her long claws scratching against the stone. "The White Fox was never satisfied. It would become real, if it had to suck the maa from every fox in the Wildlands to do so."

"But why?" I asked.

Jana sighed. "You cannot think of it as a real fox. It did not act from fox-like hopes or dreams. Always, it longed to take physical form . . . And yet in growing it could only destroy and enslave the living. It began to take shape, a ghostly being forged of ash and dust—that is why we call it the White Fox."

My throat was dry. "What happened?"

"Through darkness and fire, the Black Fox came. The other Elders took their part, sharing their maa and giving their lives so that he might live to destroy the White Fox. This ball of yearning, of unquenchable desire, was banished to the furthest edges of the sky."

"But it's just a story," said Tao too eagerly. "Something foxes tell their cubs."

Mika didn't answer.

Brin flexed his spiraling whiskers. "We do not know exactly what the Mage is doing, but . . ."

"His den lies in the Deep Forest," I said. "There are smells and strange noises. And you suspect."

Jana looked at me with ears pricked. "We suspect," she echoed softly. "Perhaps the Mage thinks he can use the White Fox to realize his power."

"If he does, he is a fool," hissed Shaya. "Once unleashed, the White Fox cannot be contained. Not by any creature. Allowed to rise, it will enslave and destroy our kind, including its former master. It will suck up our maa until there's nothing left, till the last free fox has perished. The forests will rot, the meadows will die. Even the furless will feel it."

Siffrin padded closer. His amber eyes were huge. "You can stop it, can't you?" My belly churned with fear. He usually seemed so sure of himself.

Jana watched me. "The time of greatest maa is the gloaming, when the fruit is heavy on the trees—it is our only hope of defeating the White Fox. But to do that, we need the Black Fox. And as you know, we cannot find him."

Shaya's muzzle wrinkled. "Meanwhile, the Mage is increasing his maa, pleaching without rest. If we are right—if the White Fox is rising—it may be too late by the gloaming."

"What choice do we have?" said Kolo, shaking his sandy head.

Jana's gray eyes took in Siffrin, then drifted to me. She seemed to pause in thought, her brow wrinkled with tension. She clenched and unclenched her forepaw like a cat. She looked beyond me, at the shana, and she seemed to reach a decision.

Her gaze met mine. "You did not come to the Rock to hear of our troubles." She studied me kindly. "You seek your brother."

"He's lost in the Wildlands. The Mage's skulk attacked my den, but Pirie escaped."

Jana's glance slid to Kolo.

"Why do you think he is in the Wildlands?" he asked.

My whiskers twitched. "He left the Great Snarl—the Graylands. Where else could he be?"

Mika looked thoughtful. "A fox is lost to the Elders, beyond the fur and sinew of the greatest of Canista's cubs."

My fur prickled. "That's what Siffrin said. I thought that the fox might be Pirie . . . that the 'great dog' was a wolf in the beast dens. I went there, looking for my brother. But I was wrong."

The twitter of birds; the wind in the trees. In a beat I saw Ma, Fa, and Greatma—it was almost as though they were on the Rock. Then I blinked and they disappeared. My chest tightened and I felt dizzy. I missed them so much it was hard to breathe.

Siffrin came closer. "Are you all right, Isla?"

"She's fine," said Jana sharply. Siffrin backed away a pace, looking confused, and Jana's voice softened. "She has been through a lot."

"She misses her family," said Mika, as though she'd read my thoughts.

I watched her uneasily.

"Your brother is still alive!" Mika announced, rising suddenly.

I leaped to my paws. "You've seen him? Where is he?"

Mika frowned, one long ear craned forward, the other twisted back. Her whiskers trembled like wind-ruffled grass. Her slender tail swished behind her, the white tip glowing silver. "The winds have spoken. He lives." She let out a slow breath. "I cannot say more."

My tail thrashed wildly. I was too excited to speak.

Brin cast his gaze down to his paws. After a moment, he rose and walked to the far end of the Rock, beneath the shade of the blood-bark tree. Had I somehow offended him?

Jana dipped her head. "You are wiser than your years. You suspected the wolf."

"You mean I was right?" I could hardly believe it. Farraclaw had denied any knowledge of my brother. Had he been lying?

Jana cocked her head. "Not the wolf from the Graylands. But there are others, great in number, up in the frozen north."

"No," gasped Siffrin. "She can't . . ." He took a step toward Jana, his long tail twitching.

Jana's gray eyes were locked on mine. "Mika has seen it—your brother lives. The question is, Isla, do you have what it takes to cross the Raging River? Do you dare to go to the Snowlands?"

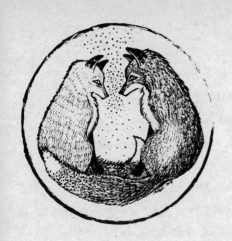

22

I remembered what Fa had told me about the snow wolves, that they ruled great kingdoms and hunted in packs. "Pirie's up there?" The idea terrified me.

"Siffrin was right," murmured Mika. "She has powerful maa."

"It takes more than maa to survive," said Shaya ominously.

Jana's ears flicked back. "Perhaps, Isla, it comes down to this: How far will you go to get what you want?"

Haiki's words leaped into my thoughts. *I'd do* anything *to get my family back.* I swiped them away. I was nothing like the gray-furred fox.

Siffrin's tail jerked up. "She can't!" he yelped. "It's too dangerous. You'd be sending Isla to her death!" His long whiskers bristled. "Where would she even start? How can she find the 'great dog' among so many wolves?"

Jana looked at me kindly. "Don't underestimate Isla's capabilities. A fox's scent will stand out in those lands."

"I can track him," I said quickly, refusing to meet Siffrin's eye. I had traveled so far since leaving my den, had searched the Graylands and the Wildlands. There was only one place left to go.

"We'll come," yipped Tao. "It will be easier to find him with three of us searching."

Jana turned to them. "You'll be too busy to travel north. Once you have learned the secrets of wa'akkir, I bid you go east to the Free Lands. Warn the skulks of the coming peril and teach them what you know, so that they may have means to fight the army of Taken."

Hope shot through me. I had feared the Elders would refuse to help us.

"Jana, will you really teach us wa'akkir?" I tried to disguise the desperation in my voice.

The gray fox's tail twitched. "Why me?"

"Because you told us about the other Elders, and their special arts. But you never mentioned your own abilities—and you never spoke of shape-shifting."

Mika snorted. "Didn't I tell you, Jana? Didn't I say she was observant?"

Shaya's ears were flat. "I don't agree with this. She's too young. Brin feels the same."

The brown fox had stretched out on his belly beneath the blood-bark tree. He didn't respond when she spoke his name. My muzzle wrinkled. I *needed* wa'akkir. Why did Brin and Shaya have to stand in my way?

I was about to protest when I saw Jana grow very still. The Elders fell silent. Their tail-tips glowed silver and I knew they were speaking without words. Even Brin sat up, alone at the edge of the Rock, as stiff as a stone. It made me think of Pirie, and gerra-sharm. Longing tugged deep in my chest. I gave myself a shake.

No . . . that path isn't safe for us.

When the light in their eyes dulled, Jana turned to me, and to Simmi and Tao by my side. "It is decided. But you must promise to respect wa'akkir's limitations—to abide by foxlore, no matter what."

My tail started wagging and I willed it to still. I needed to prove I was old enough to handle wa'akkir. I dipped my head solemnly and Simmi and Tao copied me. We quickly agreed to abide by foxlore and we waited expectantly.

Kolo limped to the shade of the blood-bark tree. Shaya followed, sitting alongside Brin. Little Mika paused, her nostrils pulsing. The fur fluttered at the base of her ears and she cocked her head. "Use it wisely, foxlings," she said at last, before turning and padding away.

Jana cleared her throat. "As we don't have much time, the lesson starts here." She drew in her breath, her ears pointed forward. "Wa'akkir is an ancient craft, a higher art. It helped our ancestors survive the brutal torments of the furless. With it you may imitate another living creature. But its rules must be strictly followed."

The sun hung lower between the trees. A raven fluttered overhead.

Jana kept talking. "You do not turn into the creature, you merely imitate it. You must only shift into a Cub of Canista—all other states are unstable. You will not appear as 'a dog,' but as a *particular* dog, not as *any* fox but as a real, living fox."

I swallowed an impatient yelp. I already knew all this—when would she teach us how to do it? I stole a glance at Siffrin. He had joined the Elders, but he didn't sit. He watched us, his long tail swishing from side to side.

Simmi and Tao gasped and I whipped around. Jana had vanished. In her place stood a vicious dog. He flashed his fangs at me and globs of spit flew from his jaws. One struck me on the nose and I shook my head in disgust. The dog began to mutter and changed back to Jana in a shiver of golden light.

The Elder's eyes bored into mine. She mouthed a few soundless words. The gray eyes remained, but her body extended, her tail shrank, and her fur became lighter. Another dog faced me—this one had a snub nose and tiny ears. His muzzle was wet and gummy.

Despite myself, I stumbled backward. "It's just an illusion!" I spat.

"Does this feel like an illusion?" the dog snarled, butting into me so hard that I toppled, breathless. Simmi yelped and ran to my side but froze as the dog wheeled toward her. "My jaws are just as strong as a real dog's. I could snap your leg like a twig." Jana started chanting, though I couldn't catch the words. With a spasm, she switched into a tiny fox cub, an innocent creature. "Be thoughtful," said the cub in a reedy voice. "There is more to wit than brute force." She skipped a short distance and started to pounce, shifting into a large male fox. She landed whiskers away from Tao, who sprang into the air with a hiss.

"Study your subject," said Jana in the shape of the male fox. "Mimic every twitch and bark." With a judder, she was herself again. The white tip of her tail glowed silver. "Think of the creature you wish to copy. Imagine her nose, her ears, her whiskers, the curve of her tail, the shape of her paw. If it helps, close your eyes." As Jana spoke, her body flickered, as though it was hardly there. The light shimmered through her gossamer fur. "Then chant," she murmured, "after me: I am the fur that ruffles your back. I am the twist and shake of your tail."

We started chanting the words together. I focused my mind on a fluffy white dog I had seen in the Great Snarl. I pictured his velvety muzzle and that strange little tail that curled up above his rump.

"Let me appear in the shape of your body: no one can tell; others will fear; dare not come near!"

"It isn't working," muttered Simmi.

I opened my eyes. She was right; she looked just the same. I studied my black forepaws, disappointed.

"Patience, foxlings." Jana was hardly there, her gray fur a glistening outline against the stone ground. "You must still your breath and focus your mind." She seemed to float just above the Rock—was that an illusion? She grew so faint that she was almost invisible.

"Like slimmering," I ventured. Wasn't wa'akkir different?

"I can't do it," grumbled Tao, his tail rising with frustration.

"Try not to push yourself—let it come naturally." Jana looked to each of us in turn. "Be careful, foxlings. Wa'akkir drains maa quicker than other arts. To stay in an altered state too long is dangerous." Something was happening as Jana spoke. Her floating form was bending, contorting. Her shimmering gray fur grew ragged. Her ears flopped down; her shoulders stooped.

She was aging before our eyes.

Soon Jana sank down onto the Rock, crumpled over like bones sheathed in fur. Her breathing grew scratchy.

"Stop!" I whimpered.

With a murmur, Jana raised her tail. The loose fur tightened at her shoulders, soft and ruffled. She looked at each of us in turn, now as a cub no older than me. "Remember, you will still smell like yourself. Your reflection will betray your true form. And you won't have a shadow at all." I noticed that the cub stood against sparkling stone. Her shadow should have stretched over the Rock—but it didn't.

I felt wary and disoriented, but my longing for wa'akkir grew stronger with every shift and change that Jana made. I did as she said, calming my breath. I murmured the chant, but my body stayed the same. "Why doesn't it work for us?" I asked.

With a jerk of her tail, Jana shifted again, returning to her old form. Her shadow seemed to cling to her gratefully. Her tail-tip still glowed silver.

"It is simple," she said. "You must invoke the creature you wish to copy. The secret is to believe—to *really* believe. When I finish the chant, I say to myself, 'I am Jana. I am changing. I am . . .'" She cast about for a moment. "'The great coyote.'" Her body juddered and a fearsome coyote spun in the air. A deep wound etched the coyote's cheek, and bite marks riddled her shoulder. This beast was a fighter.

She thumped onto the Rock with a snarl. Simmi and Tao cowered.

My temples pounded, though I knew it was Jana.

"To change back, you must reverse the shift," growled the coyote. "I am the great coyote. I am changing. I am Jana." With shivering gold and wisps of violet, the coyote spun into Jana's true shape. The Elder Fox seemed tiny by comparison. It was hard to imagine that she had the power to switch her form so rapidly.

My ears rolled forward. Could it really be that simple?

Simmi was already trying the chant, shutting her eyes, her tail wrapped around her. "I am the fur that ruffles your back. I am the twist and shake of your tail . . ." She finished by saying the words: "I am Simmi. I am changing. I am the female coyote who came to the den." We stared at her expectantly.

Nothing happened.

I shut my eyes and let my thoughts trip over the words of the chant.

Let me appear in the shape of your body: no one can tell; others will fear; dare not come near!

My eyes still shut, I added out loud: "I am Isla. I am changing. I am the fluffy white dog."

The secret is to believe —to really *believe.*

I pictured the dog from the Great Snarl, his long, white muzzle, his curling tail. I imagined what it was like to walk at the end of a rope. I wondered how it felt to have a furless touch my back. A spasm ran through me, my hairs stood on end. I opened my eyes and I looked to my paws. They were broader, with neat, short claws.

And they were white.

Simmi hissed and backed away from me. From the edge of my vision, I saw the Elders watching. Siffrin's ears were pricked.

I yelped in excitement. Then my body convulsed with a clutching pain and I dropped to my belly. As the pain drained away, I saw my paws were small and dark. My brush extended and curled around me. The shift hadn't held.

"Practice," said Jana, answering my question before I had asked it. "That is the only way."

Tao's tail was wagging. "Let me try," he implored.

Shaya was strutting toward us. "Not now," she snapped. "The sun is low. Malinta's maa is vanishing."

I gazed beyond her, to the edge of the Rock. The amber fog was thinning into mist.

"The shana cannot hold," said Shaya. "It is time to go our separate ways."

23

The sky was growing dark.

I wobbled on the frozen circle, at the edge of the cracking ice. Clumps of snow clung to my lashes. A thick pelt of white covered everything: the trees, the fence, the neighboring yard.

Only the fox stood out against the snow.

He craned his neck to stare at me. His fur was silvery but the long red hairs sprang out beneath it, vivid. Dangerous. His breath escaped his throat in misty plumes.

"Pirie!" I yelped. "Pirie, where are you?"

Water sluiced over the broken ice. It lapped at my forepaws, numbing them with its bite.

"Pirie! What should I do?"

"Your brother isn't here." The fox's voice was husky.

"He's gone for help. He'll be back any moment." I tried to sound tough but my teeth chattered. A panel of ice snapped beneath my forepaws and I recoiled just in time to see it tip and slide beneath the dark water.

There was another crack as the splinter leaped along the ice.

"Cub, come closer." The fox's amber eyes were bright against the snow.

"Keep away from me!" I hissed.

"Come here, if you want to survive! I won't hurt you . . ."

He took a step toward the bank of the frozen pond. I spat at him, losing my balance. My paws flailed against the shifting ice. The water snatched at my forelegs, dragging me into its freezing embrace.

"I'll help you. Trust me."

I blinked the snow from my lashes and stared at the fox. I found no malice in his eyes. I let him reach over the ice and close his jaws around my neck. He lifted me gently, as though I was light as a leaf. He set me down on the frozen grass. Then I bolted under the fence to our patch without looking back.

I should have looked back.

As I tried to picture the Snowlands, the memory of the frozen pond returned to me. When I lived in the safety of my family, the fox in the snow was the first stranger I'd ever known. Now I felt destined to be around strangers forever. To always question who was an enemy and who was a friend.

Twilight crept over the edges of the wood. We gathered by the roots of the blood-bark tree. Simmi and Tao were huddled together, speaking in low voices. The Elders sat in a row, their tails swaying rhythmically. Only long-legged Brin sat away from the others. He flickered in and out of view, as though slimmering absentmindedly. His gaze was fixed beyond the Rock.

I couldn't understand the change in him.

Siffrin had hardly spoken since Jana silenced him on the Rock. Now he stood in the shadows, his tail drifting low.

Simmi and Tao padded toward me.

Tao's bark-brown tail was wagging. "We're going to the Free Lands. We'll warn the skulks about the Mage, and teach them foxcraft, so they can protect themselves." He batted at me with a forepaw, nipping me gently about the ears. "Won't you come with us?" He pulled away and cocked his head. "It's the only place in the Wildlands where a fox is safe."

"I can't," I said sadly. "My brother's alive. I have to find him."

Tao glanced at Simmi. "I understand. I know it's far but . . . we'll see you again."

I nuzzled his neck. "I hope so."

Simmi licked my nose. "We'll practice wa'akkir on the

way. Slimmering and karakking too. We'll be experts soon enough." She butted my shoulder with her forehead and shuffled closer. "Take care, Isla. If any fox can face the dangers of the Snowlands, it's you. I hope you find your brother."

They said goodbye to the Elders, pausing to touch noses with Siffrin. My whiskers drooped as I watched the two young foxes slip between the trees. Simmi and Tao's journey would lead them far along the Raging River, while mine would take me over it into unknown realms.

Already, the two young foxes were concealed beyond winding foliage.

At least they have each other.

My thoughts were interrupted by Mika. "You too have a long path ahead of you." I drew in a quivering breath and tugged my gaze away.

"To a less hospitable domain," added Shaya in her cool voice. "We will give you maa, to speed you on your quest."

I looked at her uncertainly.

"Come closer," she urged. I noticed that her tail-tip was pulsing silver—that all the Elders' tails were full of light.

I did as I was told, shuffling toward Shaya. The Elders gathered behind her as Siffrin looked on. I met her eyes and was struck by the heat of her golden stare. Instantly I was lost in color. I gasped as warmth and peace rushed through me. And something else.

A blast of silver power.

It was over as soon as it started. Shaya blinked and I stumbled, released from the snare of her gaze.

My mind was awake. My legs were thrumming. I felt like I could run through the Wildlands and back, that I'd never need sleep again. Every hair on my body was tingling with heat, every muscle surging with energy.

I had never felt so awake, so *alive*. "Thank you."

Shaya was already turning. "Use it wisely," she urged over her shoulder. She stalked around the other Elders. As she passed Jana, her eyes flashed with light.

Jana blinked mildly at the auburn vixen. "Until the gloaming," she said.

But Shaya's reply was addressed to me. "The maa will fade. Then you'll truly be alone." She didn't turn as she stalked beyond the blood-bark tree. A shiver of ferns and she was gone.

Brin rose on his long legs. At last he met my eye, his curly whiskers trembling at his muzzle. "Tread lightly, young fox—run fast, be safe, live free." He didn't wait for a reply, darting between the trees without a word to the other Elders.

I stared after him, wondering what I'd missed. Why was Shaya annoyed with Jana? Why was Brin hostile?

Siffrin cleared his throat. "Isla's only a cub. She can't go to the Snowlands alone. Let me go with her." He appealed to Jana with his eyes, then shifted his gaze to Mika and Kolo.

Jana didn't reply right away. I found I was holding my breath, wondering what she'd say. For a beat her eyes glowed. "I know you want to help," she said finally. "But I need you close. You're too valuable, Siffrin. You can see Isla to the outskirts of the Elder Wood, then come and find me."

"Please, Jana."

"Sorry." Her voice was gentle but her gaze was firm. "The edge of the wood and no further."

Siffrin's tail-tip jerked but he didn't protest, and neither did I. Pirie was *my* brother—I knew it was right that I go alone.

So why was there a knot of sadness in my chest?

The sun was sinking between the bowing branches of the blood-bark tree. Jana shook her gray fur. "It is time for us to go our separate ways." She touched my nose with her own. "Tread lightly, fox—run fast, be safe, live free."

Kolo and Mika stepped up in turn, touching noses and murmuring the same words to me, to Siffrin, and to each other.

Run fast, be safe, live free.

"Until the gloaming," added Jana to the other Elders. The three old foxes trotted in separate directions, instantly melding with the shadows of the wood. I swiveled around to the Rock. The colors had vanished overhead. The stones had lost their sparkle. With the Elders gone, it was nothing special—a large plateau in a circle of trees.

I followed Siffrin as he led a path through the wood. The air was pungent with blossoms. We didn't speak as we trotted over roots and vines, winding north. I still felt the quiver of silver in my limbs, the force of the Elders' maa. I had no problem keeping up with him.

Siffrin's muzzle was low, his pace determined. His muscles rippled beneath his red coat as he moved. I wondered what he thought of me. Had he suspected Haiki all along? I pictured the Taken, trapped on the Rock. I remembered the foxes in the snatchers' den. I'd hated Siffrin for his deceptions, but perhaps I'd been too quick to judge him. It wasn't always easy to do the right thing.

It wasn't always clear what the right thing was.

We reached the outskirts of the Elder Wood. The soil turned to scrub, curving over a hill. I could hear the nearby swish of water.

Siffrin finally spoke. "You don't have to do this."

"Do what?"

He tipped his muzzle. "You don't have to travel to the Snowlands alone. Let me go with you."

Our eyes met. In those deep amber globes I caught a hint of what I'd seen in maa-sharm. The dancing colors, the soaring heat. The little cub lost, alone in the world.

"I know you think I've been dishonest," he said quietly. "I didn't mean to trick you. I should have told you about your family."

My tail-tip quivered. "It doesn't matter now."

He took a step toward me. "I would never do anything to hurt you."

I touched his nose with mine. "I know." I pulled away, padding over to the scrub. When I glanced back, Siffrin was in the same place, watching me with sad eyes.

Yearning gnawed at me. "What about Jana?"

Siffrin cocked his head. "She'll understand."

I wasn't sure that he really believed that. I hesitated, paw raised uncertainly. My ears flicked back and I wavered. "Yes," I said, surprising myself. "Come with me to the Snowlands."

Siffrin brightened and he bounded toward me. He rested his head against mine and I breathed in the richness of his coat. "I really am sorry," he said at last. "I'll do anything I can to help you find Pirie."

My whiskers tingled and relief ran through me. The truth is I'd missed Siffrin, more than I liked to admit. I needed to tell him that it was all right. That I forgave him for lying about my family; that I understood why he did it. That the Mage had ordered their deaths. That a lone fox couldn't have taken on Karka and a skulk of Taken.

That it wasn't his fault.

The words didn't come. *I'll tell him later,* I promised myself. *When we're in the Snowlands.*

Together, we rounded the hill. The twigs and roots of the wood gave way to tufty grass, then clattering shingle. I gasped in astonishment. A huge coast spread out before us.

The Raging River.

The current was furious, rolling in plumes as it charged downstream. I trod cautiously to the edge of the bank. Water crashed and frothed as far as the eye could see. A giant bird wheeled in the sky, stretching its earthy brown wings. I gazed in wonder as it tipped its white head and glared at me with piercing eyes.

The river was too huge and wild to swim across. If only we could fly, could leap into the sunset like the bird.

"What should we do?" I asked.

Siffrin let out a long breath. "I don't know." He sat, looking out over the water, and I settled by his side. The tip of his tail swept next to my paw.

He rose with a shake. "I'll see if there's another way." I watched him pad along the shingle as I listened to the crashing water. The surge of maa made me more aware of the land beneath my paws. Malinta's call had gone but I still felt a thump from the ground, a heart that beat with my own. What was Pirie doing now?

I missed my brother. I missed his voice. I missed the wildway and hunting for beetles.

You never were much of a hunter.

I sat up. Pirie had spoken through my thoughts. I knew the risks of gerra-sharm. We might be overheard. "I can't talk to you, Pirie. Not anymore."

Isla, what's wrong? Don't go so fast! I had to reach you. To tell you not to come looking for me.

My muzzle tensed. "Goodbye, Pirie."

Please, Isla. You don't understand! Stop searching. Before you go, promise me!

"I won't promise that."

I'd rather die knowing that you're alive than live knowing that you've been captured. I caught the tremble of terror in his voice.

"You're not going to die," I said firmly. "Neither of us are. We're from the Great Snarl. We've lived among the furless. Nothing a fox can do is as bad as that." The words comforted me, though I wasn't sure they were true. "I have to go, Pirie. I'm sorry . . ."

I'm scared, Isla . . . I don't even know where I am. I can't see.

"I'll be your eyes."

I can't move.

"I'll be your paws."

I feel so weak.

"I'll bring you maa. Stay strong, Pirie. I'm coming for you."

Squeezing my eyes shut, I pushed him away. The space where my brother's voice had been expanded like an echo, a great vacant nothingness. I rose to my paws, giddy with sorrow. The sun had set over the wood. My heart quickened. It was dangerous to speak to Pirie, especially at night. We'd only exchanged a few words—had anyone been listening?

I peered along the bank. Siffrin was far up the water's edge. For a moment I watched him sniff the ground as his long red brush swished behind him.

An acid tang on the air. The scratch of claws.

I whipped around.

The red-eyed foxes climbed over the hill. Their silhouettes stood out against the last whisper of silvery light. Their eyes glowed like fire.

The Taken streamed over the grass.

"Siffrin!" I cried. He didn't hear me over the crashing surf. "Siffrin!"

Already, they were sliding down the shingle.

Siffrin turned, as though by some instinct. He started running toward the Taken, cutting an arc through the cobbles. I could see his lips moving in incantation.

Shock gripped me as he morphed into a ginger cub—a cub with my face.

As the Taken caught sight of him, he'd already changed. He spun around, tearing along the bank, and the Taken pounded after him.

I reeled with giddiness, confused by the wa'akkir. But I knew why Siffrin had imitated me, and my heart thundered for him. The Taken were gaining on him, closing the gap, and I was to blame. I'd spoken to Pirie. It was only for a moment, but it was enough.

Reckless, stupid little fox.

The last of the Taken streamed down the shingle. Before I could think what to do, five other foxes climbed over the hill. Instead of chasing after Siffrin, they paused and looked around. Even from this distance, I could tell they were free foxes. Their bodies lacked the loping gait of the Taken.

My tail thrashed with relief. The Elders had found us!

Then I spotted the tips of their white fangs.

They weren't the Elders.

Five foxes of the Narral slunk toward me. Terror seized me and I yelped. The Mage's inner guard weren't fooled by Siffrin's wa'akkir. They were masters of foxcraft. And they were coming for me.

Desperately, my eyes skimmed the bank. Siffrin and the Taken were almost out of sight. When I looked back, the Narral were already at the bottom of the hill. A strange shimmer touched the air. Specks of yellow dust seeped after them, bringing the smell of decay. A dark figure stepped through the dust. He paused at the top of the hill. I'd seen him before in the Ghost Valley, though I didn't know him then.

I could make out the shape of his pointed ears, his scruffy coat.

His stump of a tail.

The Mage's eyes glowed acid blue and a low groan rose over the river. Time slowed into a thick drift. I couldn't speak, couldn't move. Could hardly breathe.

The Narral crept over the shingle. Panic flooded my senses and I stumbled backward, where the water licked the bank. Its frenzied tug almost yanked me off my paws.

Pirie's voice cut through the groan, freeing me from the Mage's enchantment.

Foxcraft, Isla!

My head shot up. The great bird had vanished in a granite sky. It was against foxlore, but what else could I do?

"I am the fur that ruffles your back. I am the twist and shake of your tail. Let me appear in the shape of your body: no one can tell; others will fear; dare not come near!"

I sucked in my breath and spoke through my thoughts.

"I am Isla. I am changing. I am the great bird."

I looked at my paws. The black fur traveled up my leg, turning ginger—just as it always did.

It's not working!

The Narral fell back on their haunches, preparing to pounce.

I yelped with fear, drew in my breath, and fought to still my panic. I shut my eyes and started chanting again.

I am the fur that ruffles your back . . .

I imagined what it was to be a bird that terrified doves

275

and sparrows, to grasp at fish with jagged talons, to slash their flesh with my beak. To live a wild, lonely life high over the world. To inspire fear in the creatures below. To see the land drop away as I tore through the air.

My body gathered into itself, powerful, furious. The Elders' maa rushed through my blood.

"I am Isla. I am changing. I *am* the great bird."

I sensed it immediately. I was different.

My eyes flicked open and I gasped.

Instead of hind paws I had clutching talons. In place of a muzzle I had a beak—a beak with the power to shatter bone. My body was sculpted of muscle and feathers. I spread my enormous wings.

The Narral cowered, whining in fear and backing toward the wood.

I raised my wings, as the bird had done in the sky, expecting them to lift me effortlessly. Nothing happened. Panic jagged through me. How did birds do it?

I struggled to steady my thoughts. In the Great Snarl, I'd seen pigeons thrash their wings as they took flight. Was it the same for a bird this size?

Fly! I told myself. I flexed my wings but they were too large to bat like a pigeon's. Up and down moved the great brown wings, but my talons stayed planted to the ground.

The Narral had paused. They glanced at each other, their fear of me already seeping away.

I loped clumsily, unable to run. If I didn't take flight, I was dead.

I gulped down my terror.

I can fly. I must fly. I will *fly.*

The Narral were creeping closer again, low to the ground.

Clumsy on my skinny legs, I started to shuffle along the shingle. I was surprised to discover that the faster I moved, the surer I felt. I pushed away the thought of the Narral close by. In my mind, I pictured the great bird soaring. By some instinct, I started to pump my wings as my talons thumped along the bank. The air caught my feathers and speeded my path. It slid beneath me and lifted me, dropping me gently back onto the ground.

It's working! I realized in amazement.

I drew in my breath and ran faster, my talons a blur of yellow, my wings great beams of brown at the edges of my vision. With a shriek of amazement, I rose into the air, slowly at first, then faster. I dashed over the foxes, my talons sweeping above their heads. Blood thundered through my body. I was flying!

I shot above the bank. The ground dropped beneath me with dizzying speed. I could see the contour of the Elder Wood. My heart screamed through my blood. My eyes widened in wonder and I soared, lost in the vivid beauty of the land below, in the thump of wings, and speed, and heat.

I was alive! My maa was silver!

I am the great bird.

It took me a moment to recall who I really was, to remember that Siffrin had fled from the Taken. I dived along the bank, watching for him, the currents of air like a stream against my belly. I could pick out the Taken toward the trees. Was Siffrin leading them through the woods? I needed a wider view.

Wind lashed my face and I drove higher, up and up into the clouds. When I dared look down, I caught my breath. The last of the Taken were no more than splotches that disappeared into the wood. I wheeled above it, a blur of dark greens and new blossoms below.

High on warm winds, I gained confidence. Silver maa crackled at the base of my feathers. I tipped my wings one way, cruising, looping, dancing patterns beneath stars.

I watched the land rush below me, no longer familiar, a new world seen from high above. I could make out the pines and the glinting cliffs. Here and there were dots of bright-globes—signs that the furless had settled deep into the Wildlands. Far in the west, beyond the meadow cast in darkness, a yellow haze hung over a forest. With a shiver, I tilted direction, watching for Siffrin's vivid pelt.

As I swooped over the Wildlands, a halo of light seized my eye—the blur of countless brightglobes. The Great Snarl sprawled across the vista, pulsing with intensity. Against the darkness of the Wildlands, it was like day trapped in night. Dipping lower, I recognized the towering buildings that shimmered like frost. Somewhere behind the snaking death-way was the patch where I'd been born, where I'd lived with my family. But that was a lifetime ago.

I turned and flew over the river. I knew that Siffrin wouldn't just leave me—he was bound to return to the bank. I spotted a red blot against the shingle. It had to be him.

I whizzed above the river toward him, my heart soaring with my mighty wings. I was lost in a space where I was wild and free. Together with Siffrin, I'd find my brother. I was full of maa—on top of the world. I flicked a look over my shoulder and caught sight of the hill. A figure still stood there banked in yellow dust. An old fox with a stump of a tail.

The Mage.

He lifted his gaze my way.

A shudder shot through me like a sickly convulsion. Pain gripped me and I cried out. My swift, sure movements broke into judders. I flapped my wings wildly but something was wrong.

Instead of feathers, a flash of fur.

Horror gripped me. The wa'akkir was broken—my body no longer the great bird's. Suddenly I was plummeting toward the rapids. My paws thrashed and I dropped, the wind screaming in my ears. In an instant, I glimpsed the lights of the Snarl, the Elder Wood, the yellow-hazed Darklands far in the east.

With a mighty splash I plunged into the river, a frenzy of paws and blinding chill. The rapids batted me, wrenched me under. I fought the current, glugging great gulps of water. The river tossed me like a leaf and buffeted me against a rock. I hugged that rock with desperate paws and dragged myself up. Straining with effort, I heaved onto a sand bank, freeing my legs of the river's grip. I gasped for every breath.

What a fool I'd been to shift into a bird! Defying foxlore, I'd almost drowned. Siffrin was back on the southern bank and I was on my own again.

But I was alive.

I had crossed the Raging River. Relief bubbled up inside me. I was going to find my brother!

I blinked the water from my eyes and the excitement drained away. A wilderness swept before me, an endless valley veiled in white. At its furthest reaches I caught the contour of snowcapped trees, and mountains that rose in giant splinters of ice. The moon was huge against deepest black. Canista's Lights were lost amid countless stars.

I shuffled onto my paws, shaking my fur. I had never felt so alone.

I must have looked strange there, a ginger speck against a sea of white. I folded my tail around my flank, feeling scared and exposed. Anyone might see me from far across the Snowlands.

Only then did I hear the haunting cries echoing over the valley.

It was the howling of wolves.

Their voices slashed the stillness of the night.

FOXCRAFT

KARAKKING

Imitating the call of other creatures. The technique allows the fox to "throw" his or her voice, so it appears to come from elsewhere. Used to attract prey or confuse attackers.

SLIMMERING

Stilling the breath and the mind to create the illusion of invisibility. Prey and predators are temporarily disoriented. Used to avoid detection.

WA'AKKIR

Shape-shifting into another creature. Misuse of wa'akkir can lead to injury or death. Its practice is subject to ritual and rites that are closely guarded by the Elders.

MAA-SHARM

Maa is the energy and essence of all living things. Maa-sharm transfers maa from one fox to another. Used to heal frail or wounded foxes.

GERRA-SHARM

Gerra is the thinking center of living beings—the mind. Gerra-sharm allows foxes to share their thoughts. It is a rare foxcraft—a forgotten art—and can only be performed by foxes with an intense, intuitive bond.

PLEACHING

The weaving of minds (gerra) with another creature. Pleaching is to the mind what wa'akkir is to the body. Its practice is perilous, as the stronger will can overwhelm and dominate the weaker.

PASHANDA

A trance state where knowledge is summoned from the winds. Used to sense the approach of friends or foes.

SHANA-SHARM

The fusing of wills to weave shana. Used by the Elders to protect the Elder Rock during malinta and the gloaming.

❧ TERMS ❧

BISHAR

A mysterious title used by snow wolves to describe their packs. Little is known to foxes of these creatures or their ways.

BLACK FOX

The ultimate master of foxcraft. An honorary title bestowed on the wisest fox—there is only one Black Fox in any age, and he or she is traditionally an Elder.

CANISTA'S LIGHTS

A constellation of stars that are the basis of a fox's maa.

DEATHWAY

Also called the death river. These are roads, but to foxes it appears as the deadliest trap of the furless.

ELDERS

A secret society of foxes dedicated to keeping foxlore and foxcraft alive. Each Elder is a master of a particular type of foxcraft—while the Black Fox is master of them all.

FOXCRAFT

Skills of cunning and guile known only to foxes. They are used in hunting or to elude the furless. Only gifted foxes will master the higher arts, such as wa'akkir.

FOXLORE

The fox's age-old struggle to survive the torments of the furless is captured in stories of resistance against all efforts to tame or destroy the fox. This lore distinguishes foxes from other cubs of Canista. Foxes understand dogs and wolves only in terms of their treachery. On one side, dogs are slaves to the furless; on the other, wolves are savages that howl to warlike gods. Foxes stand between them, answering to no one.

GERRA

The seeing, thinking center of living beings—the mind.

GLOAMING

The gloaming occurs between twilight and dawn on the longest and shortest days of the year. A time of great magic.

MAA

The energy and essence of all living things.

MALINTA

Malinta occurs twice a year, when day and night are of equal length. A time of magic.

MANGLERS

Cars. To foxes they appear as fast, growling predators with shining eyes.

SHANA

A protective field of energy.

⇥ PLACES ⇤

GRAYLANDS

The city. Also called the Great Snarl. Filled with manglers, dogs, and many other dangers.

WILDLANDS

The countryside, where many foxes live, including the Elders. Isla's fa is from here.

SNOWLANDS

The frigid northern realms where the snow wolves live, hunting in packs known as Bishars.

ABOUT THE AUTHOR

Inbali Iserles is an award-winning writer and an irrepressible animal lover. She is one of the team of authors behind the *New York Times* bestselling Survivors series, who write under the pseudonym of Erin Hunter. Her first book, *The Tygrine Cat*, won the 2008 Calderdale Children's Book of the Year Award in England. Together with its sequel, *The Tygrine Cat: On the Run*, it was listed among "50 Books Every Child Should Read" by the *Independent* newspaper.

Inbali attended Sussex and Cambridge Universities. For many years she lived in central London, where a fascination with urban foxes inspired her Foxcraft trilogy. She now lives in Cambridge, England, with her family, including her principal writing mascot, Michi, who looks like an Arctic fox and acts like a cat, but is in fact a dog.

SPIRIT ANIMALS

Discover Your Spirit Animal!

Read the Books. Play the Game.

📖 SCHOLASTIC

scholastic.com/SpiritAnimals

SCHOLASTIC, SPIRIT ANIMALS, AND ASSOCIATED LOGOS ARE TRADEMARKS AND OR REGISTERED TRADEMARKS OF SCHOLASTIC INC. ALL RIGHTS RESERVED.   SA1–7

WHAT HAPPENS WHEN YOUR MAGIC GOES UPSIDE-DOWN?

From bestselling authors **Sarah Mlynowski, Lauren Myracle, and Emily Jenkins** comes a series about magical misfits who don't fit in at their school.

SCHOLASTIC and associated logos are trademarks and/or registered trademarks of Scholastic Inc.

■SCHOLASTIC

scholastic.com/upsidedownmagic

USDMAGIC3

An epic
series
takes
flight!

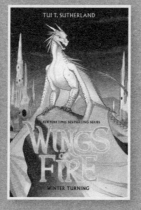

Read
them
all!

SCHOLASTIC and associated logos are trademarks
and/or registered trademarks of Scholastic Inc.

■ SCHOLASTIC
wingsoffire.scholastic.com

Available in print
and eBook editions

WINGS7